What Makes You So Special?

EDA LeSHAN

What Makes You So Special?

Dial Books for Young Readers
New York

Published by Dial Books for Young Readers
A Division of Penguin Books USA Inc.
375 Hudson Street
New York, New York 10014

Copyright © 1992 by Eda LeShan
Design by Nancy R. Leo
All rights reserved
Printed in the U.S.A.
First Edition
1 3 5 7 9 10 8 6 4 2

Library of Congress Cataloging in Publication Data
LeShan, Eda.
What makes you so special? / by Eda LeShan.
p.   cm.
Summary: Discusses the many different factors
that make each one of us a unique human being.
ISBN 0-8037-1155-7
1. Individuality—Juvenile literature.
2. Nature and nurture—Juvenile literature.
3. Child psychology—Juvenile literature.
[1. Individuality.   2. Psychology.] I. Title.
BF697.L412 1992   155.2—dc20   91-16925   CIP   AC

This book is for a frightened, sad,
angry little boy named Larry, who grew up to
be the most special person I ever knew.

A SPECIAL DEDICATION: TO FRED ROGERS

I feel quite certain that when you were much younger
than you are now, you had a very special television
friend, Fred Rogers of *Mister Rogers' Neighborhood.*
I can't think of anyone who knows more about what it
means to be a special person. I am so lucky because he and
I are friends. Even though I was a grown-up when
I watched him with my daughter, and then later got
to know him personally, he could always help me to feel
better if I was down in the dumps. When I got stuck
working on a book, he helped me get started again.
He always made me feel special.
Do you remember his songs about being special?

"You are special. . . . You are special to me. . . .
You are the only one like you. . . ."

If you watched Mr. Rogers, I hope you will always
remember how much he wanted you
TO BE YOURSELF.

Contents

Acknowledgments

How lucky I am! I have the best secretarial assistant,
Jo-Ann Straat; the best agent, Phyllis Wender;
and the best editor, Janet Chenery.
What a team! Thank you all.

Also special thanks to
Richard P. Kline, Ph.D., Associate Professor, Dept. of
Pharmacology, Columbia University, for his comments on
the chapter dealing with genetics.

Introduction

WHAT MAKES YOU SO SPECIAL?

*You will be an individual all your life;
how does that happen?*

These days it's more than likely that one of the things parents and teachers may be telling you is that you should "be yourself." Sometimes they really mean it. Other times they may say it and not mean it. When they worry about your wanting to be like other kids whom they don't admire, they say, "Be an individual—think for yourself." When they want you to do well in every subject in school, they aren't thinking about your being different, having special talents and weaknesses. They surely forget how special you are when they say things like, "Why can't you be an A student like your brother?"

As you look around at all the people you know well and famous people you just hear about, you can see that once you grow up you will become more special, more different. You will have to make so many choices about what you want to do, what to think, what to feel. It's a hard job. You will be growing up at a time when people have more choices than they have ever had before. There are baseball players who can't read a note of music; there are writers who can't understand mathematics; there are lawyers who can't swim; there are doctors who know less about state capitals than you know.

But during the next few years there are going to be many times when you won't want to be an individual, when you won't want to be different. Because you don't feel sure about yourself and can't yet realize how special you are (and wish you weren't!), it feels *so much safer* to try to be as much like your friends as you possibly can.

In nursery school, at three, you may have wanted to change your name to Alison or Daniel because that was your best friend's name.

In the third grade, you probably felt you had to have *exactly* the same T-shirt or jeans that the most popular girl or boy had.

At thirteen, everyone wants the most stylish haircut, the same goals, and the same music as the majority of schoolmates, but slowly, along the way, you begin to realize that it is impossible *not* to be different, not to be your special self.

It is one of the miracles of life that all the billions of people on earth have different fingerprints; that some people seem to be quiet and calm no matter what happens and others are always agitated and worried, even when there are no special problems. You realize that one person can paint a beautiful picture, another learn to play the violin at six, another write poems, another look at a computer and figure out how it works.

And of course there are differences that are not chosen but are just *there*—like being black or white, having curly red hair or long straight hair, being plump or skinny, tall or short. There are people who appear to be able to learn faster than anyone else, and people who have serious learning disabilities. There are people with strong, healthy bodies and people born with multiple sclerosis or cerebral palsy or other special disabilities.

There's a girl in your class whose father is an alcoholic; there are probably many boys and girls at school whose parents are divorced. There is someone with seven brothers and sisters, and someone else whose grandparents are all dead. There is a girl whose father is so rich he has three cars and a sailboat, and some other kids whose parents need food stamps and are on welfare.

No two people ever have the same family history. Pedro was born in Puerto Rico, and at home everyone speaks Spanish. William's ancestors arrived in America in the 1700's in Boston, and one of his ancestors was a president, another a governor. Jason was born with a misshapen foot; Jennifer has a curvature of her spine, just like her mother. Lester's family found out there was "radon" in the ground beneath his house; Beverly lives in an apartment house that is so big nobody knows anybody else in the building. Caroline lives on a dairy farm. Maria has never seen her parents yell at each other; Charlie's parents were always fighting until they got a divorce. Kenneth taught himself to read when he was three; Wendy has dyslexia—a way the brain works that still makes it hard to read and write even now when she is nine years old.

No matter how you all may try to be alike, so long as you are unsure and insecure about who you are, it won't work! There are too many things that are unique about you, things that happen long before you ever have a chance to make any decisions, any choices. Sooner or later you will need to recognize that you are different from anyone else, so you can make the most of being yourself.

It may help you to become most truly yourself if you know more about what makes each person different, and how you became a special person, starting before you were born. That is what this book is all about.

Chapter One

BEFORE YOU WERE BORN: THE MIRACLE OF GENES

From the moment the egg from your mother and the sperm from your father joined to begin the process of your becoming *you,* a miracle was taking place. Never before, never afterward, would there ever be a single person exactly like you, anywhere in the world. What a fantastic fact! It is hard for me to believe, for example, that with billions of people living on this planet, no two of them have exactly the same fingerprints. I have always felt that among all the mysteries and miracles of nature, this fact is the most exciting. It makes me feel that because we are all special and different, each of our lives is very precious.

Our lives begin with the facts of heredity—the "genes" we have gotten from our parents, grandparents, our ancestors. And while the facts of heredity are startling and fascinating, what makes them even more so are the ways in which heredity and environment are so closely related.

Tom and John are identical twins (created when one fertilized egg splits in two). Their mother gave them up for adoption. She was only sixteen when they were born, and she was unmarried and still in high school. She knew she wasn't ready for the responsibilities of being a mother. The adoption agency gave each child to a different couple. Tom was adopted by a family in the Midwest. His adoptive parents owned a dairy farm, and he grew up helping to run the farm. His parents adopted three other children. Tom had seven cats and two dogs. He went to a small elementary school, and even his central high school was not very big, and most of the children he knew came from homes similar to his. Tom's parents belonged to a Baptist church and his social life centered around the church. When he went to college he was amazed that there were so many people who were not at all like him or his family. The only thing Tom knew about his background was that he was adopted when he was a baby. Neither he nor his adoptive parents knew he'd had a twin brother.

John was placed in a very different environment. His adoptive parents lived in Chicago in an apartment. He was almost never allowed to go anywhere

alone until he was eleven or twelve years old because his parents were afraid he might be hurt in
traffic or get mugged. His bicycle was stolen twice
in the park when he was thirteen. His schools were
big and crowded, and there were people of all races
and religions at school and in his neighborhood.
Some were rich like his parents, others were very
poor. His father was a lawyer and his mother worked
in a bank. From as far back as he could remember
they were always fighting and they got a divorce
when John was nine years old. He was sent to
boarding schools, and during his vacations he took
turns living with his mother (and new stepfather)
and his father, who never remarried. He never went
to any religious institution—one of his adoptive
parents was Jewish, the other Presbyterian by background, but neither one belonged to any temple or
church, and religious holidays were never observed.

Nobody had given John any information about
being adopted. It came as a tremendous shock when
his parents finally told him, just before he went to
college. He was very upset that he hadn't been told
before. His parents themselves had no idea he had
a twin brother.

I'm sure you can imagine what happened! The
first day at college, standing in line to register for
their first courses, they saw each other. John said,
"It was like looking in a mirror! I felt dizzy and

scared. It seemed like some weird nightmare! It was the second big shock in a couple of weeks!"

Tom was shocked too, but not as much as John; he said, "After the first couple of minutes I felt as if this was somehow meant to happen and that I had been waiting for it to happen all of my life, without knowing why."

As they got to know each other they discovered that while there were astounding similarities, there were also major differences. They had both had measles in the same year; they both had been basketball stars in high school; their high-school girlfriends had the same name! They both had to have the same two wisdom teeth pulled when they were eighteen. However Tom was a secure and serene young man. He was very trusting, but he was also prejudiced against people of other races and religions—he'd never known any at all. He could cook and clean and was not at all anxious about taking tests. John, on the other hand, tended to be nervous; he almost never talked about his home and parents. He was suspicious of people who wanted to be friendly because he did not have much self-confidence. He often seemed to expect bad things to happen. But he got along with people who were different, and he became active in college politics, fighting for civil rights, demonstrating about pollution—and he decided to become a lawyer and eventually run for some public office.

Tom decided that rather than going back to farming he wanted to try to become a forest ranger.

Each twin, with the same genes, had had totally different life experiences that had influenced their personalities. While they both were left-handed, and both had big ears and did well in school, if they hadn't looked alike, no one would have thought they were related.

Virginia is now eighteen years old. She had not seen her birth mother, Jane, since she was four years old. Jane died at that time, and her father remarried a year later. Virginia lived with her father, stepmother, and stepbrother in several different foreign countries until she was sixteen, when the family returned to the United States and she met Jane's mother—her biological grandmother—for the first time since she was three years old.

Her grandmother is a friend of mine and she told me, "It is simply unbelievable that she is so like Jane! She looks like her, she moves like her, her speech pattern is the same; she talks very fast and gestures with her hands. She writes me the most beautiful letters, and when I compare them to the letters that Jane wrote at the same age, I have a hard time not getting confused. So many of the same feelings and talents and ideas! I have the feeling Jane is here with us in Ginny."

How could Virginia possibly be so much like the mother she did not see after the age of four? There may be some memories deep down inside of her but they are dim, and Virginia says she doesn't remember her mother at all. Their lives have been completely different. Jane lived in the same house in a quiet suburb until she got married. She had an older sister. She always knew her own grandparents very well and saw them often. The schools that Jane and Virginia went to were completely different, and Virginia could speak several languages because of the years her family lived in other countries. How could her every gesture, every facial expression, seem so familiar to her grandmother?

The reason is one of the many miracles about human beings; she had inherited many of her mother's characteristics.

Many different kinds of characteristics can be inherited. I happen to have inherited a weakness; I have a lot of difficulty learning and understanding scientific facts. My mother was just like me. We loved to read and write and study people, but math and science were our own worst subjects in school. The intricate and complicated facts of heredity are a subject you will be studying during your school years, especially in high school and college. I have tried to learn as much as I can about the subject, but what I know is far from the whole story. What I will be reporting now are those facts which seem to me to be most important in talking about what makes you special and unique.

Long before we knew very much about heredity, people observed that it was likely that each child would resemble some other relative. From the moment a baby is born, parents and grandparents will exclaim, "Oh my, that's just the way Fred looked when he was a baby!" Or after a few months someone will comment, "When Kathy turns her head and makes a face when you try to feed her something she doesn't like, she looks like that sourpuss, Uncle Frank!"

It isn't only physical characteristics that seem to run in families. My maternal grandparents wrote the most beautiful love letters to each other when my grandmother was living in New York and her fiancé was living in Austria. My mother was a very talented writer. She wrote lovely poetry, several books, and many articles. I have written more than twenty books and hundreds of articles and would rather be a writer than anything else. My two nieces and a second cousin are excellent writers. I really "got it" from both sides, because my father was also an excellent writer. There are very few good mathematicians in my family—and that surely includes me! While the environment we live in can encourage or discourage special talents or weaknesses, we are each born with our own special brain that has within it mysterious and marvelous different ways of seeing, learning, feeling.

Heredity is the passing on of traits from parents to children—eye and hair color; bone structure; intelligence; special talents, for art or music; and potential sensitivities, such as being allergic or needing glasses at an early age.

Heredity works in two ways. It makes each living thing resemble others of its kind—it never mixes up dogs and cats, elephants and dolphins, or human beings. Only cats have kittens, only dogs have puppies, and a mouse can never give birth to a rabbit. Heredity also determines what makes each living creature special within its own kind; when you watch a litter of puppies or kittens you can tell almost at once how they are different. Some are very active and others are quiet; some are the first ones to nurse, others wait more patiently. Some cry a lot, some are more cuddly than others.

Unless you have an identical twin, no one else looks exactly like you—and even twins have different personalities. All the individual variations that make us each special are caused by literally millions of different combinations of genes. The more we learn about heredity, the more we learn about individual differences.

People have tried to understand the mysteries of heredity for thousands of years, but the most dramatic progress occurred with the development of very powerful microscopes, and this has occurred only within the past century. Cells, the simplest units of living tissue, were discovered in the late nineteenth century, but as increasingly strong microscopes were invented, we learned that inside each cell there are tiny structures that were named chromosomes. And inside each chromosome were even tinier units called genes. It is the genes that determine heredity.

There are one hundred trillion cells in each person's body. There is a nucleus in the center of each cell. Inside the nucleus are the chromosomes. These chromosomes are so small that thousands of human chromosomes, if laid end to end, would be only one inch long. Looked at under a very powerful microscope, the chromosomes look like tiny bits of string, and the genes like tiny beads strung on them.

A human being has forty-six chromosomes, each of which can have hundreds of genes that determine heredity. Every person has about fifty thousand genes. Genes are made up of a chemical called deoxyribonucleic acid which is, thankfully, called DNA for short. Genes are not all equal. If you have a brown-eyed father and a blue-eyed mother, you have a better chance of having brown eyes. The brown-eyed gene is dominant (stronger). Weaker genes (like blue eyes) are called recessive genes. If both parents have blue eyes, then you will only have genes for blue eyes.

Research in the field of heredity is now advancing at such a rapid rate that, if it is a subject of great interest to you, you can surely find many valuable books in your school and public libraries (see bibliography). We are just beginning to learn how to identify some hereditary diseases and in the future may even be able to control them. We are also on the threshold of genetic studies that may make it possible to attack some diseases after birth by introducing, through blood transfusions, genes which fight these diseases.

At the same time that progress in the study of genetics has been developing so rapidly, we have also been learning a great deal about what happens to a baby during its nine months in the womb. In addition to what we inherit, we are each influenced by what happens to our mothers during pregnancy. For example, women who smoke heavily and drink a lot of alcohol and coffee often have smaller babies. Poor nutrition can affect motor coordination (the way we move our bodies) and learning abilities. Women who are drug addicts are likely to have drug-addicted babies. Women with AIDS (*A*cquired *I*mmune *De*ficiency *S*yndome) are likely to have babies with AIDS. It is now possible, through a picture called a *sonogram,* to see unborn babies, so that doctors can observe much more about what helps a baby grow well or poorly. More and more defects can be detected and sometimes cured. The study of genes has meant that we can know much more about which genes any particular child is inheriting, and doctors can now anticipate some problems a baby may have before he or she is actually born, so that measures can be taken to help such babies survive.

Not too many years ago nobody knew very much about what was going on during the nine months of pregnancy. I remember when I was a child I had a favorite aunt who always seemed to have a cigarette in one hand and glass of wine or cup of coffee in the other. I thought she was very sophisticated. Her son David was born six weeks prematurely, and in those days nurseries for "preemies" were nothing like what they are today, where even babies that weigh less than two pounds may be saved and grow up to be healthy children. For my aunt there were many weeks of worry, because David only weighed three pounds. There was no explanation for this, but today most people (surely doctors) would wonder if smoking and drinking had had something to do with David being born too soon. Of course this is not always the case. But we now know that people who smoke several packs of cigarettes a day or who are alcoholics *are* taking chances with having a healthy pregnancy and the birth of a healthy baby.

I remember my mother telling me that when she was pregnant with me, she and my father went to a lot of concerts because people had told her the baby might be influenced to love music. I thought that was the silliest thing I had ever heard. When they tried to give me piano lessons, I hated it. One day my brother heard me trying to play a lovely, delicate piece of music by Mozart, and he said, "It sounds like elephants clomping through the apartment." Musical I surely was not, but long after my mother went to those concerts, we began to learn that many things *are* going on in the uterus—that the baby responds to sounds, to a mother who is nervous or calm, to everything the mother eats and drinks. This means that we can bring important information and actions to the care of the unborn child.

While I did not become a musician because of the concerts my mother went to, my environment increased my capacity to *enjoy* music. Was it something that was related to exposure to musical sounds? Or was it the fact that a friend of mine became a ballet dancer at the Metropolitan Opera and began giving me free tickets to opera and ballet? Environmental exposure was surely a major influence, but could I have already had a readiness I never knew about?

It will be some time before such questions can be answered, but we surely are learning more every day about how heredity and environment influence our lives.

One of the most interesting studies I know of began about twenty-five years ago. The idea was to see how different children coped with the things that happened to them. Some of this work was done by Dr. Stella Chess and Dr. Thomas Alexander,* and has been carried on by many other child experts.

They and their co-workers began observing specific babies from the moment they were born. Each baby was put on an examining table. First, a bright light was shone on the infant. One baby would go right on sleeping while another baby would blink and begin to scream. Then someone would rattle the examining table a bit; one baby might give a sleepy, bubbly smile while another might make a scowling face and its arms and legs might fly in all directions.

These same babies were watched closely over many years. The first baby might have been colicky, and

---

Your Child Is a Person, Paralax Paperback, Viking, New York, 1965.

yet did not cry too often, went easily from a bottle to a cup, and toilet trained himself or herself. The second baby might well have had a difficult time learning to nurse, might have been a fussy sleeper, hated new foods, and cried hard when being left at nursery school. Babies who fussed in the early months of life tended to remain fussy or anxious or easily upset, no matter how their parents treated them. Some babies who had serious illnesses, or had a parent who deserted the family at an early age, or lived in a noisy home where a lot of fighting was going on, might stay quite serene and calm most of the time. How could this possibly happen when the environment varied so much? It is because each one was born with an entirely different nervous system, with certain strengths and weaknesses in its physiology. The environment influenced each child according to the child's physical nature.

I remember one mother telling me about her twin boys. She said that from the moment they were born, one was "easy" and one was "hard." One seemed to take life in stride, the other seemed to be battling his way through it. When they were four years old they were invited to a birthday party where each child was given a box of crayons. When they opened the boxes some of the crayons were broken. The "easy" child said, "Oh look, Mommy, I have so many more crayons." The "hard" child burst into tears because the crayons were broken.

At the extremes of differences in personality types are what I call "the wave riders" and the "wave fighters." A wave rider is the kind of child who could be swimming in an ocean with eight-foot waves after a hurricane, and would still manage to ride the waves with ease. A wave fighter is the kind of child who might be swimming in a nice calm lake but churns the waves up so much that he or she could drown! Do you have any idea where you stand on such a scale? Do you get very excited and upset easily, or are you quite calm? Or do you seem to be a little of both, depending on what is happening?

Janet and Laurie are sisters. Laurie is two years older than Janet. From the time Janet was born she always seemed nervous and agitated. She was a fussy baby, had a hard time giving up the bottle, took a long time to get toilet trained, and had tantrums when she got frustrated. She was very healthy and nothing unusual happened to her in her early years, but somehow life always seemed to be a great struggle for her. She screamed when her mother left her with a baby-sitter, and she had trouble learning to read when she started elementary school. Her father said, "Janet always expects the worst to happen!"

Laurie was born with a complicated obstruction

in her intestines. Her first operation was done when she was only four weeks old. She had to stay in the hospital from the time she was born until two weeks after the first operation. Her parents were unable to hold her or cuddle her, and she saw them for just an hour or two each day. As a tiny baby she had a great deal of pain, and most of the time she was fed through a tube.

Laurie was a bubbly, happy little girl! The nurses and doctors could not get over it. She smiled a lot, seldom cried, and when she finally went home, she adjusted easily and quickly to being with her family. When she was five years old there was another emergency and she had to be rushed to the hospital. In the ambulance, in a lot of pain, she comforted her mother, saying, "Don't look so sad, Mommy, I'll be all right."

How could this possibly be? A very excitable child with no special problems who gets easily upset and a happy, sunny, fearless child with serious health problems? Again, it is the mysterious wonder of heredity.

Despite all the unique characteristics each of us inherits through our genes, someone once commented, "Heredity is not destiny."

Even with similar hereditary tendencies, the life experiences one encounters in growing up in a family modifies what will happen. From the time that

Larry was eight or nine years old he dreamed about becoming a ballet dancer. He wanted desperately to study ballet, but his father would not hear of it. "No son of mine is going to do sissy stuff like *that!*" he shouted. Larry had a slight build and was very strong. He worked at bodybuilding but gave up his dream— he just could not fight against his father's wishes, even when he was ready to leave home. He became a high-school gym teacher, which delighted his parents.

Phillip was over six feet tall by the time he was thirteen. He too dreamed of being a ballet dancer, but it seemed about the most unlikely thing imaginable. When he was about twelve his mother took him to see a ballet where there was a dancer named Jacques D'Amboise, who was very tall and a wonderful dancer. Phillip's parents agreed to let him go to ballet school, thought it would be a fine profession if he was really talented, and for many years Phillip was a lead dancer with a well-known ballet company. He is now a ballet teacher.

Many years ago there was a great tragedy. A drug came on the market that seemed to help women who were nauseous, had trouble sleeping, and were generally uncomfortable during the early months of pregnancy. The drug was called thalidomide, and it soon became clear that it did terrible damage to the fetus. Many babies were born with severely deformed arms and legs; many had arms only to the elbow, with no hands and fingers. When Harold was born his mother almost went out of her mind. She felt terribly guilty even though she had just taken her doctor's advice about taking thalidomide. She couldn't bear to look at Harold. She cried all the time and left him in his crib a lot of the time. When doctors told her she should begin to provide him with prostheses for hands and feet, when her husband tried to teach Harold to use a crayon with his two elbows, Harold's mother cried even more. "He's a cripple," she screamed, "he can't do anything!" Harold became increasingly weak and sick and depressed, and he died from pneumonia when he was five years old.

Leo was also a thalidomide baby. His parents were brokenhearted, but from the moment he was born they told each other, "Our son is going to have a good life." They searched for experts who could help them in as many ways as possible, and they treated Leo as much like both of their normal children as possible. As Leo got older they told him, "You have the most important thing you need—a wonderful brain. You can get around your disability." Leo is now a grown man. He went to college and became a social worker and a psychological counselor. Later he also studied for the ministry and is the pastor of his church. He's married and has two children. Heredity and accidents of birth can greatly influence a person's life, but whether or not one can overcome serious obstacles depends on the kind of parents one has, and one's own attitude.

Wave riders and wave fighters are surely born with tendencies either to be calm and easygoing or to be targets for stress, anxiety, and insecurity. But that is never the end of the story. As any parent will tell you, it is much easier to raise a wave rider—a child who takes the challenges of life in stride—but sometimes these children may need a little push to make the most of themselves. Carolyn is extremely popular in school, passes all her school tests, barely makes any effort at team sports. She's so easygoing she might also be called lazy. She needs to have her parents encourage her to develop her potential abilities. She is the kind of child who will only be motivated to try to do her very best if her parents set up some rules about homework and help her to learn some physical skills.

Mitchell worries almost all the time. He worries about his schoolwork, he is scared to death of each new experience (his first carousel ride, his first day at nursery school, his first visit to the dentist). He's afraid of dogs, hates going to birthday parties, and feels shy when his parents have company. But he manages to accomplish a great deal. His schoolwork is excellent; after a few days he adjusts very well to all the new things he's scared of, and he stops worrying so much once he sees that he is doing all right.

At the age of nine he decided he wanted to go to a sleep-away camp with his best friend. All the preparations were made, and then, one week before he was to leave for camp, he changed his mind. He pleaded with his parents not to make him go. He got homesick before he went away. He cried and told his father he was too scared. His father said, "Mitchell, let's take a look at the kind of person you are. Since you were a baby you have always fussed about anything new happening to you. You got cold feet on the first day of first grade, and you still get tense and upset at the beginning of each new school year. That's just the kind of person you are. So I think you should go to camp with Robert and give it a chance. If you still hate it after two weeks, you can come home." Mitchell had a wonderful summer. When parents and teachers help a young person to understand his or her special characteristics, that child can learn to adapt, to adjust, to make the most of himself or herself.

Sometimes dealing with physical or emotional problems may call for specialized help. Charlotte was born with a clubfoot, a malformation that made it difficult to walk, and she had to have several operations before she was able to walk with only a slight limp. But she viewed her disability as something so ugly and terrible that she stayed away from other kids her own age, refused to go out to play, and thought of herself and her future as hopeless. Her doctor suggested that she join a group of other young people with special problems and eventually, after quite a struggle, Charlotte agreed to try it. She needed help in overcoming the emotional problems, her feelings about her clubfoot. I met her when she was a grown woman, married and a mother. "I was terrified to have children—I was afraid they might have clubfeet. I still saw it as an almost insurmountable problem, even after getting a great deal of help from that group. Before I got married I started to see a psychiatrist. I couldn't believe my husband could really love me—I was 'damaged goods.' It took me two years to think of myself as a *person* with many qualities, not just one not-so-good foot."

Cynthia was born with cystic fibrosis.* Chances are her life will be short; she has to have constant care and undergo very unpleasant aspirations of her lungs. But she was also born with a bright and sunny disposition. She's pretty and smiles a lot, and she accepts her life and struggles to make the most of it. She was not only born with a serious disease but with a temperament that handles it magnificently.

---

*Thick mucous forms, most often in the lungs, that must be suctioned out frequently so the person can breathe.

Beyond everyone's expectations, she is now fourteen years old, goes to a regular high school where a nurse gives her whatever special care she may need. She won an award for an essay she wrote in sixth grade about what it was like living with cystic fibrosis. She wrote, "I'm lucky to be alive, and maybe someone will find a cure before I die. Meanwhile I have as much fun as I can."

Heredity presents each of us with thousands of possibilities for what we may do with our lives. But no matter how dramatic and special our inheritance may be, the real test is what we do with what we've got.

Chapter Two

THE FIRST IMPORTANT YEARS

During the first nine months of your life, inside your mother's body, all the mysterious and wonderful possibilities were occurring in your mother's uterus. Then came the time to be born. The specialness of you became even more dramatic.

Justin's mother already had three older children when he was born. His mother was in labor for three hours and his birth was easy. His mother was relaxed, and a few hours after Justin's birth, she sat up in bed and said, "I'm ready to go home." She felt she knew exactly what to do and what to expect. "After three, there are no surprises," she said with a big smile.

Rachel's mother, Veronica, was sixteen years old when Rachel was born. Veronica had never seen her father and wasn't even sure who he was. She was a frightened, unhappy teenager who lived with a grandmother who went to work early each morning. Veronica lived in a run-down apartment house in a poor neighborhood. At school, in a classroom of forty children, nobody had paid any attention to Veronica—the teacher was too busy trying to control some pretty wild kids. When a boy in one of her classes said he loved her, she was eager to please him, she needed so much to feel loved. When she became pregnant, she was terrified. She was afraid that if she told her grandmother she would beat her. When it became clear to her teachers that Veronica was pregnant, the school guidance counselor found her a boarding home for unwed mothers. When Rachel was born, Veronica was a frightened, lonely child herself and didn't know anything about taking care of a baby. At the boarding home she had been given lessons in how to diaper and bathe a baby, but Veronica had not been close to any baby before and had hardly ever had a chance to be a baby herself. She told me, "You can't imagine how dumb and how scared I was! There was an older woman in the room with me and when they took her to the delivery room I heard a nurse say, 'Be sure and take her teeth out.' I got totally hysterical! I thought they were going to take my teeth out—that maybe that was something they did when a person had a baby. I jumped out of bed, screaming, and tried to run away.

It took two nurses to catch me and hold me down so they could explain that the woman had false teeth and they were afraid she'd choke on them!"

Rachel's mother was in labor for fourteen hours. There was no relative or friend to help her. When Rachel was born, Veronica didn't want to see her or hold her—she was too scared. Rachel was placed in a foster home where there were four babies. Most of the time she was left alone in a crib. She cried a lot. Her mother went back to school and later got a job. Rachel didn't go to live with her mother until she was two years old. By then she was a very angry, frightened little girl.

Mai Ling was born on a Red Cross cot in a tent among refugees from a country in Southeast Asia. Her mother was very quiet and never complained and had big sad eyes. Her husband and older child had drowned when they were escaping. Her mother was exhausted, sick, and pregnant when she finally got to the refugee camp. She was so sad she didn't much care if she lived or died. Other women in the camp nursed Mai Ling's mother and took care of her for three months until she began to recover. When Mai Ling was a year and a half she and her mother came to the United States. Mai Ling was shy, quiet, and frightened for a long time, until she got to know her uncle and cousins.

Bill's parents were so overjoyed when his mother

became pregnant with him. His parents had wanted a baby for many years. His father was with his mother all the time in the delivery room. His mother had to have a cesarean section, which means that Bill was born by an operation that allowed the doctor to bring him into the world through his mother's abdomen. He was born very quickly without any struggle. This is occasionally necessary when it seems the baby might have too hard a time being born through the mother's vagina. To his parents Bill was the greatest miracle of their lives, and they argued with each other about taking turns holding him! They were nervous about taking care of a baby, but too happy to think about that very much. All they did was look at him and marvel and kiss him.

Vin's parents, Mark and Charlotte, joined a special class for expectant parents, when his mother was seven months pregnant. Mark and Charlotte had read many books on birth and babies and chose a doctor who would be on call for his birth, which would take place at home, where a midwife would help with the delivery. Mark and Charlotte had been taught all the ways in which they could help Vin be born. Charlotte's mother, Mark's two sisters, and Charlotte's best friend were all in the room when Vin was born. There was great rejoicing and singing, and some champagne. Vin began nursing very soon after he was born.

Maybe your mother was in labor for fifteen hours and had a hard time while you were struggling to be born. Maybe your father was too scared to stay in the birthing room and paced outside in the hall, or fell asleep on a couch. Maybe you were born so fast that your parents never made it to the hospital; they had to call 911 for instructions until the ambulance came.

While each baby already has inherited differences in personality, each one also is greatly influenced by how its birth has taken place. Mai Ling might naturally be a baby who was likely to be calm and easygoing, but what happened to her in the beginning of her life might make her anxious. Vin might be born with a tendency to be very excitable and even nervous, but the experience of his birth might have a very calming effect on him.

No matter what the combination of genes and chromosomes may be in the makeup of each baby, there is surely *no way* babies can ever turn out to be exactly like any other babies. Every child is born to his or her own special parents, the world they live in, their attitudes and feelings, their particular relatives, and all their life experiences. There is no way you can avoid being special and different, because it started from the moment you were conceived, when you inherited your unique physical history, and continued to the unique experiences of your birth. This is why, later, it can be *such a struggle* to try to be exactly like the kids you admire the most!

There are, however, certain ways in which all children are alike. They all have some similar feelings during the first few years. The reason for this is that we all go through the same very important stages. These stages affect us differently, but they remain the common bond of all people everywhere. Following are some of the things you share with your classmates, your parents, your teachers, your grandparents, your aunts and uncles, your neighbors—in fact with people all over the world.

When a baby is born it responds most of all to sound and touch. It can't think in words. A baby can't say, for example, "I feel lonely and wet and I wish someone would come and hold me." All alone in a crib, a baby feels only a general sense of comfort, or of unhappiness. A baby doesn't know anything about time or space. A baby can't figure out that there are other rooms in an apartment or house. A baby has no sense of time. An infant doesn't know that sooner or later someone will come and take care of it. These feelings can be frightening—a feeling all over a baby's body. There is no way to say, "I am scared." When daddy puts the baby in water that is too hot, the baby is furious. It screams and kicks its legs and arms. The anger is all over its whole body—the baby can't say, "Hey, cut that out!" When mommy doesn't come quickly enough to nurse or give the baby a bottle, the baby gets angry all over without being able to say, "What's the matter with you? I'm hungry, snap it up!"

Needing to be touched and fed are the first things that all human beings have in common. The second thing is that we all started to *feel* without being able to put our feelings into *words*. It's not easy to be a baby! We all want grown-ups to understand how we feel because we can't tell them. If grown-ups don't understand, it will be very hard to get over feelings of pain and anxiety.

Max's mother has twin girls just a year and a half older than he, and she's so busy he can feel hungry for what feels like forever before she gets around to feeding him. Being hungry is something he won't remember later on, but he may turn out to be a person who gets very mad if he has to wait too long for a meal in a restaurant!

Jessica's father walks up and down, up and down, for hours, holding Jessica, patting her back, singing to her when she has a pain in her stomach—which happens very often during the first three months of her life. She suffers from colic, and only feels some relief when she is rocked or held. It is possible that when she gets a cold or the flu later on, or has to have her tonsils taken out, she will want her father to be with her every second. She doesn't remember those nights long ago but somewhere deep inside her is the feeling that only her daddy knows how to make her feel better.

And there is the sad—even terrible—fact that some parents are too unhappy, too immature, to be able to take good care of a baby who might be crying a lot, and they may scream and hit the baby. We know that unless these children get a great deal of help from other people, they may grow up with so much misery and anger inside them that they too may hurt other people.

Another very important thing we all had in common as infants is that we thought that anything that happened was our fault, and wanted so much to be loved that we would do anything to try to please our parents or other people who took care of us.

When Keith was about two years old he began having temper tantrums—he would just get so upset he would kick and scream and throw toys and maybe even kick his mother. It so happens that almost all children go through a "tantrum stage." The reason is that there are so many things you want to be able to do, so many ways in which you want to be more independent, and there you are, with very few skills and still needing to be taken care of all the time. It is extremely frustrating! If you were lucky and someone said, "I know how upset you are, and

I'll stay right here with you until you feel better—all little children feel this way sometimes," you could think, *Well, I guess I'm not a bad kid, I'm just little.* And as you got older you could feel pretty good about yourself. But just suppose a mother or father spanked a child hard and said, "You're a *bad boy*—go to your room and don't come out until you can behave yourself." How would that child feel? Very likely this child would believe that he really *was* a bad boy, and unlovable. And if other things happened that resulted in his being punished and told he was bad, he would feel that, because parents are supposed to know everything and be wise, he must really be a rotten kid. Unless someone can begin to explain that all little children do things they should not do (like biting or hitting or spitting) and that these kinds of behavior are normal at certain stages of growing, children go on feeling naughty and guilty. What all children need to hear is that children can't control their childish impulses, and that they need help from grown-ups. They are not bad—they are just young and need help until they can control themselves. All little children have common needs and feelings and behave in similar ways, but one of the things that makes each child very different is how grown-ups treat them.

Another thing all children have in common is thinking that only they themselves have angry feelings and are afraid. There is no way a child can know he or she is just like other children, unless someone talks about this. Joshua is three years old, and he has this terrible fear that a lion is going to escape from the zoo and eat him up. When he lies in bed at night he is so scared that every noise makes him feel as if the lion is coming to his house. He keeps calling his mother and crying. His mother is tired and cranky and says, "Stop this nonsense, do you hear me? There are no lions—you're just being a big baby!" Joshua decides that his mother thinks he's a coward and he feels very ashamed. He decides there is something wrong with him.

On the other hand, Susan is terrified of horses and has nightmares about being stomped on by a horse. She also calls her mother. But Susan's mother says, "Most little kids are afraid of something—animals or thunder—or even the sound of a vacuum cleaner! Tell me a story about this horse."

Susan says, "He's very big and strong and you never know what he might do. One minute he's gentle and nice and the next minute he gets crazy and jumps around and gallops and makes noises. I never know what makes him change or what he will do next."

Susan's mother smiled. She said, "Does that horse sound like anyone we know?" Susan looked very puzzled. Her mother turned on the lamp, took a piece of paper and a crayon and drew a picture of a horse who had a face of a man wearing glasses and was scowling.

Susan was puzzled, and then suddenly she laughed. *"That's Daddy!"* she said.

Then she and her mother talked about Daddy having a bad temper and never being sure when he was going to get angry and how that scared Susan. Her mother said, "He's just blowing off steam. He has a very hard job, and when he comes home sometimes he's very irritable and tired. He's not really mad at us, he's probably mad at his boss but has to be very polite to him." Susan was learning that her fear really had to do with her father. Human beings often transfer uncomfortable feelings to another person or to an animal.

The way we feel about ourselves depends very much on whether grown-ups make us feel bad about being angry or fearful, or whether they help us to understand that such feelings are normal. And children need help in understanding that there are no feelings we can't talk about, but there *are* some feelings we have to learn to control—someone has to stop us from hurting other people or ourselves. It's normal to be jealous of a new baby sister, but it is absolutely forbidden to drown her in the bathtub! It's normal to want a bicycle someone else is playing with in nursery school, but bopping the rider over the head with a block is not allowed! Feelings are normal, but some actions cannot be permitted. This is something that is very hard to learn, and all human beings worry about not being perfect. When grown-ups explain that these feelings are normal, children feel reassured. They feel safe; if they can't stop themselves from hurting others, grown-ups will always keep them from expressing angry feelings in actions that are dangerous or unkind.

All human beings share worries and confusion about what it means to be a good person or a bad person. It is hard for a young child to realize people are not either entirely good or bad, wonderful or terrible, lovable or unlovable. We are all a mixture of a thousand different feelings. We just have to learn not to hurt ourselves or other people. That's the most important thing we ever have to learn—not to be angry at ourselves, not to feel we are failing because we aren't perfect, but to learn to control our behavior.

The fact that parents and other adults react in very different ways to our feelings and behavior is another reason why each of us is "one-of-a-kind," and different from anyone else.

A normal, common reaction of most two-year-olds, when they feel frustrated, is biting. You want Mom to let you go outside without your boots—you bite her hand; or your big sister takes your truck and you bite her. So far, you are like most other two-year-olds. But one mother is so furious she bites back and pushes her child away. Another mother says, "Oh, no, honey, you are not allowed to bite. Biting hurts too much. We won't let anybody bite you, and when you're angry you tell me and we will try to fix whatever is the matter. I'll have to remind you, and I want you to look at my face. I am *very* upset." While some feelings and actions are the same, attitudes depend on how a child is treated. Unfortunately, some children get the idea that they are "bad," and fortunately, some children get the idea that they are just little and will still be loved and guided, whatever they do.

Attitudes about being special in one way or another are learned over a long period of time through many repeated experiences. Pablo feels in being bad he is different from others, because his father beats him with a leather belt. Pablo grows up hating himself, and with a terrible hidden anger at his father. Like most children, he blames himself for being badly treated and takes his feelings of guilt and anger and self-hatred out on other kids by fighting all the time.

Geraldine's parents are kind and caring and make her feel she's a wonderful little girl. If they feel they have to punish her, she understands it's to help her remember which things she can do and which she can't. She grows up never wanting to hit anyone.

These are extreme examples, but they make it clear that children may have some common qualities, but becoming different from other people depends on our experiences, for better or worse.

At a very early age, when many important things are happening, children are too young and inexperienced to understand all that is going on. Bruce's father gets very annoyed when Bruce is afraid of going into the water at a lake. His father says, "Last year you loved the water—now you're acting like a baby again!" Bruce feels he has disappointed his father, that there is something wrong with him. What neither he nor his father understands is that two-year-olds aren't afraid of the water because they're not smart enough to know about drowning! A three-year-old knows you can slip and go underwater and not be able to breathe. He's old enough to sense danger. His attitude about himself will depend a good deal on whether his father ridicules him or understands that actually he is being more cautious because he now has had more experience.

Barbara's mother screams at her for not wanting to finish her lunch. Her mother says, "You better finish what's on your plate or I'm not going to take you to the playground." Neither Barbara nor her mother understands that Barbara really can't eat anymore; most children need less food between about three and four years old than they are given to eat. But Barbara has made her mother angry and she feels like a really bad kid. She gets the idea that her mother can only love her if she eats more than she wants to eat. Young children always blame themselves because they think their parents are always right. Maybe you can't believe you ever felt that way, but you did!

I bet that sounds pretty funny to you now. By the time a child gets to be seven or eight he or she knows parents are far from perfect—they don't know everything, they make mistakes, and they don't always understand things. But by the time kids "wise up" they are likely to have strong feelings about themselves based on the attitudes of grown-ups, which started when they were much younger.

Adam is ten years old and feels so embarrassed because he is still scared of swimming in the ocean. He has learned to swim very well in the YMCA pool, but when his family goes to the beach, he won't go into the ocean, even though he suffers when his family or other kids tease him. Adam has no idea why he is so frightened of the waves. He doesn't remember, but when he was two years old an uncle who was a teenager carried him into the deep water at the ocean and let go of him because he thought a child could learn to swim that way. It was a terrifying experience, and when he was choking and crying, his uncle got frightened and felt guilty, and never told anyone what he had done.

When children are very young, things happen to them that they cannot remember when they get older, and the more upsetting and frightening the experience might have been, the less likely they are to remember.

Brooke is eleven, and many of the girls in her class are getting to like boys a lot. They may pretend not to, but they giggle and flirt and talk about boys half the night at pajama parties. Brooke can't understand why she is afraid of boys and doesn't want to have anything to do with them. What she does not remember is that when she was four years old a boy who lived in the house next to hers took her down in his basement, made her take off her panties, and began poking her with a stick. When she cried and tried to run away, he began hitting her with the stick. Someday, when she's older and might eventually talk to a psychologist about her fear of boys and men, the counselor might help her to remember what happened, so she can begin to conquer her fears.

Elizabeth can't stop herself from eating sweets all day. She started comforting herself with sweets when she was about three and her father left her and her mother and got a divorce and didn't seem to care about seeing her very often. Eating soothed her hurt, angry feelings. Elizabeth is now fourteen years old and, oh, how she wishes she could go on a diet! But no matter how she tries, she desperately wants candy after failing a test in school, or not being chosen for the hockey team because she's too fat and clumsy. She has no idea why she has such cravings. Perhaps someday someone will help her to remember how sad she was when she was three and how much she wanted to be loved and taken care of. When her mother had to work even on weekends, Elizabeth would stay home and eat boxes of Mallomars and Hershey bars instead of playing with other children.

Trevor, at ten, is still afraid of thunder. He feels like an idiot and is very ashamed of himself. He tries to pretend he's okay but he shakes inside. How could that be when he already knows the scientific explanation of thunder and knows it can't hurt him? When Trevor was three years old, his father, who is a stern man and who felt he had to teach Trevor to be brave, punished Trevor if he cried during a storm. He told Trevor he was acting like a baby and was to stop crying at once. Because Trevor wanted more than anything else to please his father, he forced himself to stop crying, but he couldn't stop feeling scared. Trevor thinks there must be something wrong with him. There isn't. When any grown-up tells a child who is very young and frightened that he or she should not "act like a baby," the fears often recur until we learn where they began.

Jenny gets bad headaches and stomachaches very often in the morning before she goes to school. She feels sick when anyone is mean to her. She gets a headache if a teacher scolds her. She gets a stomachache when her parents have to go on a trip and leave her at home with her baby-sitter. These aches and pains started somewhere along about three or four when Jenny got the idea that no matter how she tried, she could never satisfy her parents. She could tell that her mother was disappointed because Jenny wasn't pretty enough, and her father got so exasperated when she couldn't learn to catch a ball, and no matter what she was doing they were always correcting her and saying, "We know you can do better than that." This kind of pressure—feeling you can't live up to your parents' expectations—can affect you physically, and Jenny is still trying too hard to become a perfect child, because otherwise she feels she is unlovable.

The truth of the matter is that almost all parents say things and do things that upset young children—not because they are mean but because they may not understand the feelings of little children. One of the most important things they may not understand is that little kids blame themselves for anything and everything that happens. They think it's their fault if parents fight; they think it's their fault if they wet the bed; they think it's their fault if they can't remember the alphabet and forget how to tie their shoes. The truth is that all that's wrong is that they are young, that they are little, and that growing is different for each child. The truth is that no child is ever responsible for the problems of grown-ups.

The more frightening and upsetting an event (or many experiences) may be in early childhood, the more likely it is to be forgotten. This is called "re-pression," which means that what has happened is too painful and the mind just doesn't want to re-member it.

Another thing all children have in common is that when they learn to think in words, some pretty scary events sometimes happen. Words seem magical and powerful. If you say, "I love you, Grandma," she hugs and kisses you; if you say, "I won't, I won't!" all the smiles disappear from the faces of the grown-ups around you. Words affect people so much. As language begins, it seems to a child to have magic qualities. If words can influence how people react to you, can words make bad things happen? When a young child gets very angry and thinks, *I wish my mother would go away forever and I'd never have to have my hair washed again!* he or she gets terribly frightened. Maybe the words can make something bad happen. Children need to be taught that thoughts do not make things happen; only actions can. One of the hard jobs for children, from about three to five, is to learn that words may affect people's reactions, and actions can be dangerous sometimes, but *thoughts* are perfectly safe.

When my daughter was about four years old she got very angry at me one night when I told her she had to go to bed. She yelled, "I wish you'd go away and never come back—but don't you dare go downstairs!"

Little children, up to the age of about five, are almost totally dependent; they must be taken care of by adults. They want so much to be loved that they try terribly hard to be "good." Each child becomes special because, while all children may have common feelings, the way they are treated by grown-ups influences each life in different ways. Children whose parents remember how they felt when they were young can explain normal feelings and behave in a kind and understanding way. Feeling good about oneself is not only influenced by how your parents and other relatives treat you, but also by their hopes and dreams for what kind of person you will be.

Later on, as children get older, they begin to understand that it is just about impossible to live up to these hopes and dreams. They begin to understand it is not their fault. They begin to realize that parents are far from perfect. They may even realize that their parents may still be trying to please *their* parents—and how hard that can be. Oscar's father works for his grandfather selling electrical supplies. He heard his father telling his mother, "I wish I'd had the courage to tell my father I wanted to become a history teacher." Alison's mother would love to stay home all the time and take care of her children. Alison hears her mother talking to a friend on the phone. She says, "My father is driving me crazy. He can't stand it that I want to be with my babies all the time. He keeps complaining—why did he bother to let me go to Harvard if I wasn't going to use my brain? He wants to pay for sitters so I can go to law school. I keep asking him, 'What's the big rush,' but he makes me feel guilty."

What we have been learning over many years is that "selling out" is a bad idea, because in addition to suffering ourselves, we cannot make other people happy if we are unhappy. Sometimes even when a person loves his or her parents a lot and doesn't want to hurt their feelings, a time may come when it is necessary to say, "I love you, I know you want the best for me, but I have to try to be myself." This is much too difficult when children are very young. But as we grow we can begin to see how living in a family influences us and nothing can stop the process that makes us more and more special.

Chapter Three

LIFE WITH FAMILY
❧

When I was in second grade we studied the cave men—our prehistoric ancestors. I must have been fascinated because sixty years later I can remember the pictures of these strange-looking people, and every picture showed adults and children together, whether they were eating some kind of plants or learning to use fire, or climbing trees, or hunting tigers, or sleeping in a cave. From the beginning of human time, there seems to have been an instinct for being in a family. Of course not just human beings but many other creatures as well—tigers, lions, monkeys, dogs and cats, ducks, and hundreds of other kinds of males and females—take care of their babies until they are old enough to take care of themselves. The word "family" tells us about something that every human being has in common; we all want and need to be part of a family.

Sometimes we learn the most about how important families are to children, from sad and serious problems. Anthony's father died in a car accident when Anthony was four years old. He has six brothers and two sisters. His mother tried as hard as she could to keep her family together after her husband was killed, but she was frail and sick. After his father's death, Anthony's mother began crying all the time, could not get herself to go to work, or buy food or help her children. She just sat in a chair in a dark corner. Anthony could not understand what was happening, but later, when he was older, he realized his mother must have had a nervous breakdown from too much stress, too many problems. When Anthony was six, social workers came and took all the children to three different foster homes. His mother was taken to a psychiatric hospital.

When Anthony told me this story he was twenty-seven years old. He cried as if his heart was still breaking. He said, "I remember it as if it was yesterday. When we realized what was happening, all of us children went bananas. The older kids tried to hit the social workers, and the two littlest kids hung on to my mother's legs, screaming, and had to be pulled away. I remember riding in a car and looking out the back window and seeing the other kids getting into another car and a station wagon, crying. Only the two oldest ones went to the same place. From that time until they sent me to reform school when I was twelve, I never saw my brothers and sisters."

The reason Anthony was sent to reform school was that he was never able to adjust to foster homes. Inside he was so angry and hurt at what had happened that he began failing school, refusing to behave, and joined a gang and began stealing.

Two of Anthony's brothers finished high school and have good jobs; Anthony and one sister and one brother have spent time in prison. I met Anthony at a place called The Fortune Society, where he was getting counseling to try to repair the damage of his childhood. He said, "Nothing worse can happen to a kid than losing his family. Somebody should have helped us stay together until our mother got better and we got old enough to go to work. It is a terrible thing not to have a family. Now I get together with some of my sisters and brothers whenever I can, but it is as if we are all like soldiers who were hurt in a war and will never get healed."

Many people feel it is a terrible thing to separate brothers and sisters, and most social agencies in charge of children from troubled families now try to provide a housekeeper or a single foster home.

Phyllis's parents were divorced when she was six. Her mother remarried a year later, and Phyllis's stepfather scared her half to death. Sometimes he beat her and sometimes he would secretly slip into her room at night and say she had to touch his body and let him touch hers—or he would tell her mother she should be sent away. Phyllis kept quiet for two reasons. One is that when the most terrible things like child abuse occur, children blame themselves. Of course children are *never* responsible for awful things happening, but they feel that way anyway. The other reason, as Phyllis explains it now that she is a grown woman and is getting help from a therapist, is, "I needed to be with my mother. My father never came to see me. I had only half a family, and there was *no way* I would take a chance of being sent away. Just knowing that I had a house to go home to after school, no matter how scared I was, seemed much better than no home at all."

When I was a child I loved to have my father tell me about how, in 1902 when he was six years old, he came to America from Russia with his mother. His father and older brothers and sisters had emigrated when he was a baby. When they came into New York harbor, his mother pointed at a rowboat. It came alongside the ship as they were reaching Ellis Island, where all immigrants were taken for processing before being allowed into the United

States. His mother said, "There is your father and your two sisters and your five brothers." My father was frightened. These were all strangers to him. But he found that there was so much love, such a strong family feeling, that after awhile he knew that he and his family would always be together. As I grew up, the family got bigger and bigger and when they met at weddings or anniversary parties—or funerals—I always felt how wonderful it was to be loved by so many people.

During the great depression of the 1930's, when millions of people were out of work, families struggled as hard as they could to stay together, but sometimes they were separated when the older children or the parents desperately tried to earn money for food. A friend of mine told me that when she was nine years old her father left her and her mother and two brothers. It was a terrible shock—she had been so sure he loved her. Many years later her mother explained that he had gone away in search of work. He wanted his family to have all of the food they needed while he worked as a cook. When he finally came back to his family he was very sick and soon died. "My father became a sick old man from traveling and from not being with us," she said. "Now that I am grown-up, I live in terror of ever being poor again." Life is not too different today from those hard times in the 1930's, with too many families trying to stick together in shelters, or all sleeping in a car because they can't find work or places to live.

When World War II began and London was being bombed every night, many English parents decided that they had to protect their children by sending them to rural areas where it was safer than in the cities. The government found families that would take the children and paid for their care. Some children were even sent to other countries—some came to Canada and the United States. It didn't work at all; the children were so upset about being separated from their families that eventually the experiment was given up. The children preferred to go down into bomb shelters in basements and subways at night and sleep with their parents. They were less scared of being hurt or even killed than they were of being sent away from their parents.

This universal common need for being connected, for being part of a family, is something that all human beings share; it is a need that makes us all alike in one way. But because each family is made up of different, unique individuals having different experiences, family life is also the place where we each become more special. Each of you has a family style which is unique in many ways.

Gary lives on a large farm in Iowa. His family raises dairy cattle. He has three brothers and two sisters. An aunt and one grandparent live with the family. There are also three farm workers living in a bunkhouse and eating all their meals with the family. The men are often up before dawn and work hard all day. Gary's mother, his two sisters, and the wife of one of the farm workers do all the cooking for all these people. They also do all the laundry and shopping. The boys mow the lawn and chop wood. Gary's family lives the way thousands of farm families used to for centuries in this country. His family's life-style has almost disappeared altogether, as big corporations buy up more and more of the land. The cost of farming today is too high for most individual small farmers.

Ronald lives in New York City. By the time he was born his parents had bought a house called a "brownstone," built in the late 1800's or early 1900's. There were thousands of such three-story private homes at the beginning of the twentieth century. His father's parents have an apartment on the top floor. He has one brother and one sister. There is a housekeeper who lives with the family and helps his mother, who stays at home most of the time, although she is also a volunteer worker in a hospital and has several charities for which she helps raise money. Ronald's father owns a dress factory. Ronald's family lives the way thousands of families once lived in New York City. Most of the quite-beautiful brownstone houses now have one or more separate apartments on each floor. Many have been allowed to get very run-down. Very few families now live the way Ronald does. It's gotten to be too expensive for one family to take care of a private house, and the taxes have gotten too high. Today, millions more people are crowding into cities where there is not enough housing for them, so some owners began to turn their brownstones into small apartment buildings.

Ronald's family life is exactly the way I once lived, except that my family lived on the top floor and my grandparents, aunts, one uncle, and one or two other relatives lived in the rest of the house. I went back to see the house recently, and now there are eight apartments listed on the front door. My grandfather's garden, where he raised a few fruit trees, is now a parking lot. I keep wondering how that beautiful place with its carved stairways and high ceilings and big rooms must have been changed.

Today there are more choices for many families, but there are also families that don't seem to have any more options than families of the past. These are usually poor people who have not had a chance to get much education. Julio's family works long backbreaking days in the lettuce fields of California for very little money. Little children work along with their parents. Marguerita's family lives in a tenement house in a crowded, noisy neighborhood, the only place her family could afford when they came from Puerto Rico. There are rats in the apartment, the toilet is not working properly, and there is a leak from the apartment upstairs. Marguerita sees drunks, drug addicts, and prostitutes every day in the hallways. She and her parents are scared all the time. That is surely not a life that any family would choose.

Gregory and his sister Camille and their parents have been sleeping in their car most of the time for three months. Once or twice a week they go to a shelter where they can sleep on cots and take a bath and get some extra food. Until this year, both their parents worked in a factory. They rented a small house in a nice neighborhood. They had plenty of food and clothes, a big color TV set, and once a week they went to a movie and then had some pizza. But the factory closed and their parents had no money saved. Although there was nothing he could have done about losing his job, their father felt that he was a terrible failure. He was a proud man who had never asked anybody for help; now his wife has to go ask for food stamps and go to the welfare department and stand in line to get government surplus foods, like cheese and bread.

In some ways fewer families have as many choices as they might have had a few years ago. For example, many women who would like to stay home with their children cannot. Living has become so expensive that both parents have to work, and of course, single mothers have to support their children. However, with all these exceptions of people caught in traps they never created, more people choose their own particular way of living than ever before. Some families feel that appearances are very important and they always dress in expensive, stylish clothes; some families seem to live in blue jeans almost all the time. Some families eat at fast-food restaurants a lot and at home they eat lots of meat and fried foods. Some families spend a lot of money at health-food stores on vitamins, and many have become vegetarians. Some families stay very close to their relatives and see them all the time, while other families may only see close relatives once or twice a year—or not at all. Some families spend all the money they have while others save some money every week, no matter what. Some families take their children to zoos, museums, the ballet, theater, or to visit historic places on vacations, while others try to get to a seashore or to mountains and forests for vacations.

Some families will borrow money to take the children to Disneyland, while others may spend as much money on buying a computer that children can use for homework. Some families go to church every week, some only go on important holidays, some have private ideas about right and wrong and the mysteries of the universe and have their own private religion. Some families teach their children that certain people who are different are bad and dangerous; other families try hard to see good qualities in all people. I have never met two families who had exactly the same ideas and exactly the same goals.

By the time you were born, so many couples were getting divorces that perhaps you grew up with the constant anxiety that it could happen to your family. Every time mothers and fathers have an argument their children get frightened that they are going to get a divorce. Almost half of you have lived through a divorce. There is surely no longer an attitude that women must stay home and only men must work. Surely too it is better that women have the right to do interesting things with their own lives, but children are usually not as enthusiastic about this as many parents may be. Despite the problems, many of you are proud of your parents, even though both parents are working outside the home, which makes life pretty complicated and even frenzied sometimes. Many of you are grateful that because both of your parents have jobs, you are able to have a ten-speed bicycle and go to camp and maybe even have a swimming pool. Some of you know that if both of your parents didn't have jobs, they might not have enough money to pay the rent and buy food and clothes. In spite of all this, when I ask young people how they feel about the new kind of family life, many say they wish a parent was home when they got home from school, and they wish their parents weren't so tired all the time. There are some good things about the new kinds of families, and there are some things that are hard on children.

Families have always been disrupted by the death of a parent. I may not have heard anything about divorces when I was a child, but I knew many, many families in which a parent had died and the other remarried; stepparents and stepchildren were as common, I guess, as they are today. In the past medical care was much more primitive. Many more women died in childbirth, and many men died of heart attacks, because we knew so little about diet and health. We now have so many new medicines and procedures for saving lives, and many once-fatal diseases, such as smallpox and polio, have been eliminated for the most part.

My mother's mother died when my mother was four years old. When her father remarried, she soon had two stepsisters and a stepbrother. Because her own grandmother had died quite young, her grandfather had remarried also. Many families had similar histories. The thing was, however, that the new family groups stayed very close, and of course no one could be held responsible for dying. Divorce is different, in that those of you who have lived through it and those of you who worry about it often do blame parents; some of you even feel responsible yourselves, which of course is totally untrue, but it is a normal feeling that many young people have. Death is something that just happens; divorce is something people choose, and that can make it much harder for children.

When I was a child I truly believed that human beings always took care of their children until they were old enough to leave home. During my entire childhood, I don't remember any family I knew in which there was a divorce.

Families did just about everything together. I didn't eat in a restaurant until I was ten or eleven years old. I never went to a movie without a grown-up until I was about thirteen. There were no fast-food restaurants, no drive-in movies, no places where kids could go by themselves. It may sound terrible to you, but I was very happy. I had a very big family, and we visited relatives a lot. Parents had more time to read and play—there was no place to go. Most of us had parents who watched over us very carefully. There were far fewer people, and whether in city neighborhoods or in farm areas, adults watched out for each other's children. (There were practically no suburbs then, but there were lots of small towns.)

For most of human history, married people had been teams—they really could not survive without each other. This was especially true when most people lived on farms, and there was no way they could survive without everyone doing his or her share of work. Before there were microwave ovens, frozen foods, vacuum cleaners, washing machines, refrigerators, take-out food chains, food processors, and a thousand other kinds of household equipment, there was no time for anybody to think about whether or not they were happy. It was assumed life was hard and you just did the best you could to survive.

I can remember a time when we had a great big kettle on the stove for heating water and washing the clothes, and people rubbing clothes on a washboard, until their hands were sore, to get the laundry clean. I remember waiting for the iceman to come and having to empty the drip pans under the icebox. Everything we ate was cooked at home, including bread and birthday cakes. Without television, whatever brief moments of recreation families had, they had to make their own fun. We played games and older people read us stories—and with so much work, people went to bed very early. My father's two sisters went to work in a lace factory when they were thirteen and fourteen years old, six days a week. Most children had no time for play—little kids of eleven or twelve had to work in coal mines. When I was a teenager, I went to Albany, the capital of New York State, to hear the legislators fight for child labor laws. When new laws were passed, children were required to stay in school until they were at least sixteen years old, as they are today.

When there began to be machinery that could do the work faster and more easily, people had more time to think about whether or not they were happy. At the same time the study of psychology was increasing, and there were new kinds of experts who were concerned with what made people happy or unhappy. When marriage was no longer an absolute necessity for family survival, people began to think much more about being happy, and of not putting up with severe problems. And when the women's movement began, the roles of men and women changed so rapidly that for many people there has been confusion and uncertainty about how to make the best use of the new equality between the sexes.

Each of us needs to feel there is one place where we are always loved and welcome, no matter what. I think the family is the best place for children to learn to feel loved and appreciated, and where they can learn to love others and to become civilized, caring adults. In my many years of talking and working with families, I have reached the conclusion that in most cases people who grow up most able to lead useful and satisfying lives are those who have been carefully guided by loving parents.

Of course some divorces are absolutely necessary and many of you know that. If your parents are divorced, you may have seen one parent in a drunken rage beat you or your siblings, or you may know of a parent who rarely came home, or parents who screamed and fought all the time. Although some divorces may be necessary, it hurts a lot when a family breaks apart.

Some good things about the modern age are that most divorced people remarry, and the new family may turn out very well; that grandparents are now trying harder than ever to stay close to the grandchildren when their children divorce; and that there are many places where children of divorce can sit down with other children and a counselor to talk about their feelings. Rhiannon's father left her mother and her when she was three years old, and now, in fourth grade at school, she meets once a week with a counselor and with other children of divorced families to talk about their anger and their pain, which helps a lot. Now there are books for young people to read to help them understand the normal feelings of fear and anger and hurt (see bibliography).

More than ever before, families can choose how many children they want to have, as better birth control methods have been developed. Years ago there was a very popular book, *Cheaper by the Dozen.* Large families were much more common when there was less information about family planning, and people lived in big houses and household help was very cheap. When I was born in the 1920's, people were beginning to think about how many children they could afford to raise. Now, hopefully, more and more people will limit the number of children they have, because they will think about the population explosion and what can happen when there are billions of people who will have to live on the resources of this planet. This is one of the good new choices.

Look around your class, where almost everyone is trying to be exactly like everyone else; Toa is Mexican and moved to the United States two years ago; Ian's great-grandparents have been living in America for three generations. Avram just joined your class—he's a Russian Jewish refugee. Celeste's family came here from France after World War II, and her father works for a French newspaper. Edgar's father lost his job a few weeks ago, and Edgar is too worried to be able to do his schoolwork.

Ten kids in your class live with their single mothers. Ray has a heart condition and can never take gym. Louis's father is in prison because he was selling drugs. Nicholas's mother is a congresswoman and is on television very often. There are probably some kids who have a grandparent sleeping in their bedroom. Another girl or boy you know has a mother who drinks too much—no one can ever be invited to Anita's house. Some children live in one apartment three days a week and in another four days a week, because their parents have joint custody. Emily's father died a year ago; Aileen has never been to a dentist; Dianna has braces. Colin's parents travel almost all the time, and next year they are going to send him to boarding school; Ramon never sees either of his parents, who live in Jamaica, an island in the Caribbean. He was born when they were both teenagers, and he lives with his grandmother in the city. Pamela's parents have a beautiful house on a lake and two cars, and Pamela takes ballet and piano lessons.

As you go around your classroom, you will of course find many more variations than I have mentioned. It may be that learning more about your classmates will shock you. You may have thought that if all the boys used the same swear words and wore jeans with holes in the same place and acted as if they hated girls, you would all be alike. No such luck! And maybe the girls thought that making their hair look as if it hadn't been combed for two months and pretending they hated math would make them all alike. No such luck!

Because of your heredity and the experiences of your birth and your family differences, you will have to face the reality you don't enjoy right now—because you don't want to be different right now—that whether you like it or not, you are special!

So far I have been mentioning mostly the facts about family life. Even more important in being special is how parents and children feel about their experiences in living in a family.

Sam's father's attitude about discipline is to beat a child with a belt every time he's "bad." He treats Sam the way his father treated him. The problem is that being treated cruelly turned Sam's father into a cruel and unthinking person too. Although he *thought* his father was right and he was just a bad kid, inside, deep down, he must have been very angry. Now that anger is expressed against Sam, and when Sam goes to school his teachers worry about him. At a conference with the school psychologist his fourth-grade teacher says, "Sam is angry all the time. He's like a volcano that might erupt at any moment. The children are afraid of him and so am I."

Juanita's mother and father are quiet, gentle people who would never knowingly hurt anyone. When they feel that Juanita needs to be disciplined for doing something, like running into the street or hitting another child or bringing things home from school that don't belong to her, they explain why these things are wrong and that someday Juanita will be able to remember not to do such things. They tell her she must sit down and think about why she can't do whatever she has done, and if it's something serious, she may have to stay indoors after school or not watch television for a week. Her parents make it clear they love her and that's why they have to teach her what is right and wrong.

Juanita knows she is lovable, and by being cared for in such a kind way she is able to care for other people. When Ariel falls off a swing in the school playground, Juanita runs over to comfort her and takes her to the nurse's office. When Bernard's father moves out of the house, Juanita sits next to him on the school bus and pats his hand.

Parents and other adults teach us how to behave by the way they behave. The more understanding and kind a parent is, the more understanding and kind a child will become as he or she grows up.

I often meet and talk with groups of parents. At one meeting a mother told this story:

> I was standing at one end of my kitchen peeling potatoes. Roy and Karen, eight and four,

were arguing at the other end of the room. Suddenly Roy hit Karen. I was *furious*—how dare he hit someone younger? And, even worse, he had a smirk on his face—I sure wanted to give him a good smack. I started to yell at him, and then suddenly—it was like an electric light bulb going off in my head—I remembered that when I was a kid and I did something for which I felt guilty, I would get that funny smile on my face. So what I told Roy was that I knew he felt very bad about what he had done, and that I wanted him to apologize to Karen and then go to his room to think about it for half an hour. Roy had such a look of gratitude and relief it was hard for me not to laugh. I was so glad I was able to remember how I'd felt.

From my point of view that was excellent discipline. Roy's mother was understanding, but she also made it clear hitting was not allowed.

There is another way some parents discipline their children, which I call "the making of monsters!" This happens when parents are unable to discipline their children at all. They have misunderstood ideas about kinder discipline and think it means never scolding or punishing children at all. I went to a picnic once where the father allowed his young children to pour sand on the steaks that were being barbecued in the yard. He laughed nervously and said, "I guess they are pretending that's salt." We guests were furious. Sometimes we have had people visit us with their children who are so wild, so uncontrolled, that when they leave we never want to see them again—as we pick up broken dishes, wipe up spilled milk, try to sew up a tear in a couch cushion. Parents who don't discipline their children are hurting them almost as much as the parent who thinks hitting is a good idea. By being too easygoing, too permissive, they are allowing their children to behave in ways that make others feel very unfriendly toward them, which is not the way children really want other people to feel about them. Childlike behavior is normal, but that doesn't mean children can do mean or dangerous things.

The ways in which parents discipline their children is one of the things that makes each person different. Each parent has different dreams and hopes for their children. Some parents believe that children should have a chance to grow slowly, play a lot, not worry too much about learning to read and write. Other parents feel it is never too early to start teaching as much as possible. Parents also have very different attitudes about taking care of children. Mollie is an only child, born to her parents long after they had given up hope of having a baby. They were older than most of the parents of Mollie's friends. Mollie is their precious jewel; they worry about her night and day. They never let her go beyond the fence around their house, they never let her run and climb because she might get hurt. It is almost impossible for Mollie to grow and become more independent.

Marcus and his five brothers and three sisters are practically always on their own, in a rough neighborhood. Each one has had to learn to fight and to protect himself or herself, and their brothers and sisters. Their parents work in a hotel as a chambermaid and a busboy, where there are long hours, and they are too exhausted to pay much attention to their children. Marcus told me that by the time he was seven he "was a man," a wild street kid who had learned some things about life that his immigrant parents who didn't speak much English would have been horrified to hear.

Nathan and Sophie spend lots of time with their parents. While both parents work hard during the week, they make enough money so that weekends and vacations are planned for the whole family to be together. The parents have many friends, lots of interests, and what they care about most is being a happy and loving family. They expect Sophie and Nathan to argue and fight some of the time, but to get along most of the time.

Parents' attitudes toward men and women are

different in each family. Lewis's parents share all the household chores. His father took care of him at least half the time when he was an infant. When his mother has evening meetings, his father puts on an apron, does the dishes, takes care of the laundry. Carmen's mother works three nights a week cleaning offices so that she will be home with her children during the day. Her mother would rather not work outside the home at all, but she has to. Over the weekends she teaches her two daughters to cook and clean while Carmen's father rests. Her mother truly hopes her children will have enough money to stay home and be full-time housewives, which she feels is the most important job a woman can have.

Each parent has a totally different personal history, different childhood experiences, and different personalities. This is often very confusing to children, but it helps us learn that we have to respond to people in different ways. Some parents try hard to present a "united front." They want to agree about how to raise children, but no matter how they try, children learn they are different.

When I was a little girl my mother would come into my room on a Saturday morning and sweep everything off the shelves onto the floor and say I couldn't go out until I cleaned up my room. I remember being furious and shaking my fist and saying, "I will never treat a child this way!" Lo and behold, my mother had such a great influence on me that I began doing the same thing to my daughter, Wendy. As soon as I started yelling, my husband would come into the room and say, "Mom is acting a little crazy—let's go to the playground until she calms down." Actually I was relieved because I didn't want to do what my mother had done.

On the other hand, Wendy, like most children, went through a stage of terrible table manners and kicking the legs of the table. Her father would yell, *"Wendy! Civilize Up!"* Wendy would come in the kitchen, and I would explain that when Daddy was a child his family made a tremendous fuss about table manners. My family never made a big deal about it—they were sure we would get over being restless and noisy while eating.

My parents invited interesting people to have dinner at our house and we wanted to hear what they had to say, so we learned how to behave. At Wendy's father's house every meal was a nightmare of fussing about table manners. So that still bothered him as an adult, while I was bothered about keeping rooms cleaned up. Attitudes of parents depend on what they experienced and learned when they were children.

Sometimes families have really serious problems, especially if teenage children become very rebellious and are difficult. For young people this is a period of rapid growth—hormones becoming active, a lot of fears about the future, feeling uncomfortable in changing bodies, wanting desperately to be popular, often feeling exposed to dangerous temptations to "be like other kids." Parents become terrified about drugs, drinking and driving, and sexual experimentation. Teenagers are scared but don't want anyone to know, and at the same time they feel they must rebel against their parents if they are going to grow up. Adolescence tends to be a rough time for most families. Some families get help from family therapists. Some parents become so frightened and desperate that they decide to try "tough love," kicking the kids out of the house. I believe this a very bad idea. I wanted my daughter to know that no matter what happened, no matter what trouble she might get into, we would always stick by her—that we had to solve problems in the family. Of course, if young people do start taking drugs or drinking, or if a girl becomes pregnant or a son doesn't use a condom in this time of terror about AIDS, parents have to call on community resources—people and social agencies—to help. But it seems to me that abandoning a child is never the answer.

Different approaches to problems surely create different feelings and attitudes—and influence your personality.

When strangers came to visit when you were little, were you relaxed and friendly or nervous and shy? When you went to first grade the first day, were you scared you would never learn to read and write or did you feel confident everything would be all right? When you have to go to the doctor for shots do you worry and feel like crying, or do you say to yourself, *It will only last a second and it won't hurt much*? If your parents go away on a vacation and leave you with grandparents or sitters you love to be with, do you worry about them and wish they hadn't gone, or do you hardly think about it? There can be many reasons for having different reactions, but one reason may be that you are just "that kind of person."

This is also true about parents' personalities. One parent may enjoy a noisy, active child; another may have a better time with a quiet child. What a parent is like himself or herself plays a part. One mother says, "I was such a tomboy, and my mother wanted me to be cute and pretty and like a little doll. I love having a rambunctious kid! She's having the fun I never had." Or a mother with the same background might say, "I can't help myself; much as I hated not being allowed to wear blue jeans and play rough games, I find myself doing the same thing to my child that my mother did to me. I can't seem to help myself."

Part of your unique and special self has to do

with the background of your parents—what happened to them when they were young. The happier they were, the more likely it is that they will enjoy being parents and will have a good deal of common sense; they won't be too nervous about being parents. The more unhappy a parent's childhood may have been, the harder it is to be a successful parent.

There is a nursery school which is for battered children and their parents. When parents are accused in a court of abusing their children, they are not sent to prison. They are "paroled" to this nursery school, which they must attend with their children! This school has teachers who understand little children and give them a great deal of love. They treat the parents the way they treat the children, with lots of love and understanding. The parents begin to feel cared for and in turn can begin to care for their children in a new and better way. The idea behind this program is that if parents themselves had a very unhappy life and not enough loving care when they were children, they have a very hard time being loving and caring to their own children.

There is one thing many parents don't realize, and that is that the children who are hardest to raise almost always turn out to be very wonderful grownups; they tend to become leaders and to be very successful. Gentler, more easygoing children are special in their own way—perhaps capable of being warmer, more loving, having more friends, wonderful at helping other people. There is no way of knowing exactly how a child will turn out, but if parents seem to get more exasperated with you than a brother or a sister, that doesn't mean you won't be a terrific grown-up. You may be the kind of child who can't wait to grow up. Such children long to be able to make their own decisions and follow their special talents. How many times have I heard parents say, "My daughter drove me crazy when she was a child! What a mouth on that fresh kid! Now she's a famous criminal lawyer!" Or, on the other hand, a parent will say, "Lorraine was such a mousy little kid! So shy it drove me crazy. Can you imagine—now she works with disabled children, and she's so gentle and loving, the children adore her!" Parents do not have crystal balls; they are not fortune-tellers—and neither are you! The very things that may worry you or your parents about you now may be the qualities that will give you the most satisfaction and success when you are an adult.

If you live in a family in which a parent is an alcoholic or a drug addict, the special problems show right on the surface. The most important thing for you to understand is that you are never, in any way, responsible for such problems, and you have every right to ask for help wherever you feel you can get it—from an aunt, or a school guidance counselor, or asking to go to an Al-Anon meeting.

There is one serious problem that is much harder to recognize and can sometimes interfere with your becoming your best special self. When a parent is mentally ill, it may not be so obvious and therefore harder for you to know what is happening. Mental illness is having special kinds of physical and emotional problems that are very severe—such a person desperately needs expert help.

Gabriel's mother can be so charming and delightful—singing in the kitchen, laughing hilariously over some game or a TV comedy, ready for a picnic at a moment's notice. Then, suddenly, Gabriel will wake up some morning, and when he goes into the kitchen for breakfast he is shocked to find his mother weeping, not able to explain why, telling him to get his own breakfast. When Gabriel comes home from school his mother is sitting in the dark living room, just staring into space. The house is a mess, there is no food for supper. His father is very nervous and upset but doesn't say anything. He buys some food, cooks supper, just says, "Mom isn't feeling well." Probably she will then stay in bed for several weeks. All this seems very strange, as if there is no reason for what is happening. Gabriel's mother has a mental illness. She is a "manic-depressive." That means her moods change drastically without her being able to do anything about it. If Gabriel's father says nothing, does nothing, just waits for the "bad times" to go away, Gabriel can grow up a very worried and frightened person. If, on the other hand, Gabriel's father faces the problem and takes his wife for psychiatric and medical help and explains what is happening, Gabriel won't feel guilty, and although he can still feel frightened, other people can help him understand and deal with this problem. If his mother can talk to him about her feelings and explain how certain medications are helping her, Gabriel will grow up feeling hopeful about learning new things and will be eager to help.

I have been talking mostly about problems in living in a family. Home can also be the place where you can take your troubles and be comforted. It is a place where you can feel safer than anywhere else in the world. It is a place where people are truly concerned about your welfare. It is a place where someone brings you chicken soup and a comic book when you have the flu. It is the place where we begin to learn that while human beings can get angry, scream, cry, laugh, be patient or impatient, understanding or mean, sooner or later everyone recovers from the bad times, and there can be wonderful times you will never forget—like a camping trip where it rained all the time and the tent collapsed, or a trip to Disneyland, or the whole family sitting, beaming, while you act in a school play.

A new and wonderful thing happening to many families is that we are learning to talk about problems and to get help in solving them. It was once common for a child who got beaten every day never to tell anyone; today, more and more children understand this is cruel and unacceptable treatment and that they have the right to let other adults know about it. More and more children are learning to understand their own feelings and the feelings of those around them. When my mother was a child, she was taught that it was wrong to feel jealous, and only bad girls were rude and she must never get angry. When she had a tantrum she was so severely scolded that she never got over thinking she was not as wonderful and lovable as she really was.

One of the good things that came to be in my lifetime was a much greater awareness of how difficult it is to grow up and how human it is to fail—and to keep trying to become a more mature person. And next to awareness is the wonderful fact that *families can now get help*. Even small towns, and surely every big city, have experts to help families figure out what to do when they are in trouble. One of the new "inventions" which I never heard of until about ten or fifteen years ago is what we now call "family therapy," in which every member of the family sits down with a counselor and learns new and better—and more honest—ways of relating to each other.

This is especially important if one child in the family seems to be causing all the trouble. What we have learned is that this child is a "bell ringer"— that he or she is trying to get some attention for a whole family that is in trouble. The people who behave in ways that seem to be the worst are the ones begging for help, and not just for themselves. They are the children who somehow are able to recognize what is happening to the whole family that is disturbing and needs healing.

Living in families that are so different from each other in so many important ways means that by the time you start elementary school and want so much to be as much like your classmates as possible, you will have some battle on your hands! In the early years of growing up when we feel insecure, uncertain, when we find such variations in skills, when we fear failure, it is so hard to cover up our differences and act as if it were possible *not* to be special. How can children take all the differences of the earliest years of family life and take that special self into a classroom and all try to be alike? That's a major problem, and I fear that few schools focus their attention on specialness but rather on similarities. From elementary school through high school, the struggle between being alike and being different goes on. I always hope that specialness will win out, but it's not an easy matter.

Chapter Four

LIFE IN SCHOOL

When you start going to elementary school, there are likely to be three things on your mind. One: Will you feel homesick? Two: Will you be popular? Three: Will you be able to learn the skills you are being sent to school to master—reading, writing, and mathematics?

Because of your heredity, your life experiences, and your personality, your school experiences will be different from anyone else's. And because you are in the particular school you go to, your experiences will be different from those of children in other schools.

Sometimes you will love going to school. Mitsuko's first-grade teacher is young and pretty and very gentle. Sometimes you will hate school. Julius has a fourth-grade teacher who ridicules any person in the class who doesn't get a long-division problem right. He's very sarcastic, and the only time he smiles is when he piles on weekend homework. Sometimes school will open up new doors and help you to feel powerful; you discover you know more than your parents about things like the ecology of the ocean, and where Zambia is, and how to measure triangles. Sometimes school can be very disappointing. When my daughter came home from her first day in school, she was crying. "I didn't learn how to read or write!" she sobbed. Many children go to school expecting miracles to happen.

From the moment you start your formal education, your life continues to be influenced by what has already happened to you.

Eliot actually began "school" when he was six weeks old. His mother is a lawyer, and the law firm she worked for didn't believe in giving women maternity leave for more than six weeks. His mother did not want to lose the job she loved and where she could earn an excellent salary. There was no way that Eliot could let his mother know how much he missed her and how frightened he was at first, having strangers take care of him. Later on, Eliot couldn't remember that he was allowed to lie in his crib for long periods and that he felt lonely; he needed more cuddling and holding than he was getting. By the time his father came to pick him up

(Eliot was in a day-care center from eight in the morning until six at night.), the noise and the people had made him tired and cranky. He cried a lot at home, and since his parents were also tired after a day at work, they fed him and put him to bed and looked angry when he cried. By the time he went to kindergarten, Eliot was very quiet. His teacher said he was withdrawn, that he didn't often reach out to play with other children. By the time he was in fifth grade, his teacher said he had "burnout," meaning he'd gotten sick and tired of always being with other people.

Whatever qualities Eliot might have been born with, his personality had surely been influenced by what happened to him. Suppose we imagine a different story for Eliot: Let's imagine that when he was born he had an older brother and a sister who were already in school. His mother had wanted another baby because she just couldn't bear not having an infant to take care of; maybe she had felt sad when the other two children had gone off to school. This Eliot's mother was happiest at home being a mother. She was sure Eliot would be her last baby and she couldn't bear to leave him with sitters, and spent almost all her time with him. When they went to the playground, she worried every minute about his getting hurt. She just couldn't bear to send him to nursery school, and so this Eliot didn't have much chance to play with other children. His mother hovered over him so much that he began to be an angry boy who was being smothered by too much attention. When he finally got to school, he was kind of drunk with power; his mother wasn't watching him every minute, and so he became quite rebellious. He didn't pay attention to the teacher, because now the most important thing to him was playing with other children. He had a lot of trouble learning to read and write—he just wanted to play rough, exciting games all the time.

Jeanette lives in a suburb of Chicago. She lives in an area where families have enough money to live comfortably and most of them have school-age children. When her parents hear that the school tax is going up, they pay it willingly, because they moved to this community so that Jeanette could go to one of the best schools in the country—small classes, excellent teachers. A large variety of subjects are offered, including art and music. Jeanette loves going to school.

Jerome lives in a poverty-stricken section of Chicago where the school is overcrowded. There are so many children with serious problems that most of his teachers are too tired and harassed to pay much attention to him. He's scared of the big, tough kids, who fight and who make him give them his lunch money. He's also having trouble seeing the blackboard, but he feels his mother doesn't have money for glasses, and he's too scared to tell the teacher he needs to sit up front. Jerome hates school.

Kevin goes to a private prep school. His parents are very ambitious and want him to be an A student. Kevin's parents and teachers meet quite frequently. If he gets a C, he has to go to tutoring classes. He feels tired and angry because he has to work so hard. He wishes he could go to a public school where there weren't so many kids smarter than he thinks he is. Often he dreads going to school.

I sometimes wonder what sort of person I would have become if I had gone to a different kind of school. I had a lot of trouble learning some subjects. I got nervous about not doing well, and I couldn't think too quickly. Flash cards with words on them terrified me, and mathematics was a nightmare. If I had gone to a very strict school where marks were very important, I would have failed. I surely would have thought I would never amount to anything because I was "dumb."

But that didn't happen to me. When I was growing up there were quite a few experimental schools where educators were trying new ways of teaching. Mostly this was "learning by doing" through interesting projects, lots of trips and adventures. In my school there were very small classes, and while I had trouble with some subjects, I was a great success in other ways. There were art classes, and I discovered I loved to work with clay. I made some sculptures that are still in my home and are often admired. There were special classes in writing and dramatics, and I was a great success there too. I had a biology teacher and a French teacher who let me know that even though I was in their slowest classes, they felt I was a talented person in other ways, and I knew they liked me a lot. By the time I graduated from high school, I knew what things I could do well, and I knew that it didn't matter that I wasn't as smart as other people in subjects that were either hard for me or which I found boring. I had spent twelve years in a wonderful school. Some of my classmates are still my best friends. I recently went to the fiftieth reunion of my class, and I realized how very lucky I had been, because those years had helped me to feel good about myself. What happens to us during our school years has a lot to do with how we feel about ourselves.

My husband went to an elementary school and high school where marks were the only important thing. He was a sad, unhappy, angry little boy because his parents fought with each other all the time. He just couldn't concentrate, and he failed year after year. Nobody knew what to do with him; they just passed him along from grade to grade. In those days (over sixty years ago) there were no school counselors, no extracurricular subjects. What he did was spend all his free time in the library, where he found books that got him excited and interested. His teachers could not have imagined that he was reading adult books at the same time he was failing in school. The library was his secret school where he could learn what he wanted to learn. He kept on failing until the second year of college when he discovered psychology—the beginning of a brilliant career. It is very clear now that he was a bright child who was too unhappy to concentrate in school. We now understand that unhappy children need schools with teachers and counselors who understand their emotional problems.

There have always been some brilliant teachers, like the great Greek philosopher, Socrates, from 2,500 years ago, but public schools for all children were started only about 150 years ago. The main reason then for sending children to school was to teach them a few simple skills so that they would be able to live and work as adults. Most of the United States consisted of rural farms 150 years ago. The school term depended on when parents needed the children to do work on the farms. That's why the school vacation is still in the summer. Children were needed at home to help with planting and harvesting crops on the farm. Schools were one-room schoolhouses for children of all ages, because farms were usually fairly far apart and the children had to walk to school. Most schools had about twenty children or fewer, with one teacher who usually boarded with one of the farm families. Can you imagine such a school? Sometimes I wish we still had one-room school-houses. The lessons were easier than they are today, and older children helped the younger ones. It was like a family of brothers and sisters. Most of what children needed to learn in earlier times could be covered by the time they were about twelve years old! Poor children in cities went to work by the time they were ten or twelve. Very rich city kids had tutors or went to private schools. Nobody thought children should be able to read and write until they were about seven years old.

Of course in farm areas, villages, towns, and cities there were variations in what was being taught, but the population was much lower than today, so classes were small and fewer subjects were taught. Imagine going to schools that never heard of electricity or telephones or flying or X rays. I remember trying to memorize all the elements that make up the earth, such as iron, oxygen, sodium, or silver, when I was in college; now the number of elements discovered since then has almost doubled. If you think of the inventions of the last half-century alone, you begin to realize how much less children had to learn in earlier times. And can you imagine a time when there were no organized team sports, no intelligence tests, and little emphasis on grades?

Of course in much earlier times there were exceptional students, like Thomas Jefferson, who went to college, or people like Abe Lincoln and Benjamin Franklin, who learned mostly through their own reading rather than in school. People could become doctors and lawyers by studying on their own. There were often no state licenses, no formal requirements or exams to be passed. Sounds great? Today would you want to go to a doctor who was "self-taught?" There has been such an explosion of information in every area of life that now we want doctors to know literally thousands of new facts and techniques and to practice medicine in ways nobody could have dreamed of one hundred or even fifty years ago. Young people feel much more stress and pressure to learn a great deal very well. The problem for students is that human nature—the time one needs to grow and learn—hasn't really changed, but schools have changed, demanding more and faster learning.

Some school buildings are so old and decrepit that fuses blow every day if the teachers try to install computers, or even television sets. Some schools—most of them—were built for fewer students than are crowded into them now, because the population has grown so rapidly. The majority of teachers don't have enough of the materials they need to teach effectively in these overcrowded schools, and in too many places a curriculum that may have been adequate fifty years ago is now almost useless. One teacher told me, "Can you imagine trying to teach about rockets in a school that has two Bunsen burners and a sink in the science lab?"

Today's schools frequently are not set up to include offices for guidance counselors, athletic directors, gyms, or medical supplies for emergencies. A father told me, "We are not giving Gilbert permission to play football because there isn't any emergency medical equipment in his school, and a nurse is only there three days a week." Now that we know so much more about differences in the way children learn, we also need schools that have special teachers and equipment for children with learning problems. Now that parents of so many children are divorced, and so many mothers must work, and more than half of all parents need the income of two working parents, we need schools that can care for children after three o'clock. We need after-school recreation programs, clubs, sports, supervision. Now that so many adults have to work all day, we need schools and staff that stay open evenings, for teacher-parent conferences, classes for adults, ways in which people who didn't finish high school can do so now. With people of so many languages and backgrounds, we need more classes for learning English.

With new dangers in crowded neighborhoods we need more school guards and police officers. We need hot lunch programs for children who live in welfare hotels or shelters and do not have a healthy diet and, therefore, cannot learn as well as children who have homes and good food. But most parents find that taxes are already too high, and they don't want to pay more to get better schools. It is therefore very hard to change schools, to see that they provide the teachers and equipment needed in today's world.

Some educators believe that schools should just teach academic subjects and almost nothing else. Others believe that schools should help children learn about art and music and many other subjects. Some experts believe that competition is very important to prepare young people for life later on; grades and sports are emphasized. Other educators believe (as I do) that schools should help young people explore every aspect of life in order to become the best adults they can possibly become, and that means greater emphasis on self-understanding and caring about each other.

If the goal in your school is to teach you all the same things, this can lead to problems. People who feel anxious about not succeeding at what others see as important can begin to have unhappy feelings. In a school where all the test results are pinned up on the wall, there is likely to be more jealousy and rivalry, more feelings of extreme pride and extreme failure. This doesn't exactly encourage real friendships.

Most of you, I'm sure, have lived through both the pain and the pleasure of scapegoating. It is what happens when young people feel insecure, so two kids gang up on a third in order to feel strong. The "victim" keeps changing, which is a good thing to remember. Getting together with one friend and saying mean things about a former friend, or teasing the current outcast, makes the team of two feel safe and more self-confident. The only trouble is that a week later the outsider may become the favored one, and you may be excluded. Because there is so much competition in most schools and because each person does not yet have strong feelings of his or her worthiness, it is important to watch for those times when classmates act in ways that eventually make everyone unhappy.

Your education depends not only on the people in your school, but on boards of education and government legislatures. There never seems to be enough money for schools, even though it seems to me that a child's education is far more important than building new roads or weapons. One of the things that has always made me extremely angry is that when schools are in financial trouble and budgets have to be cut, the first things to go will be things like the school orchestra and classes in understanding human emotions and special teachers to help children who have some kind of learning problems. Social workers, people who try hard to help the families of school children, are likely to be among the first people fired—and who, I think, are needed as much as teachers. When you have trouble learning, or have other school problems, it is not your fault. It means the school is not helping you enough.

There are very few communities in this country that pay teachers nearly as much money as sanitation workers or bus drivers—both of whom provide important services, but who are not required to go to school for such a long time.

There are teachers who knew from the time when they were very young that the greatest joy for them would be to be with children and help them learn. There are teachers who chose teaching so they could have the same hours as their children, and who hope someday to do something else. There are teachers who prefer a smaller income than they might get in other jobs but like to have long vacations and pensions and security. None of these are necessarily the wrong reasons for becoming a teacher, and the large majority are happy in knowing they are doing just about the most important job there is. In a very few cases people may choose teaching for the wrong reasons. Ms. Wallace had seven brothers and sisters that she had to take care of every day, so she never could play with her own friends. She grew up hating children, and a lot of her anger is expressed in her classroom. Mr. Gardner grew up in a family where both his parents were alcoholics and where he lived in terror of their fights. He grew up scared of everything and somehow got the idea that a school would be the only place where nobody would notice him too much. And, unfortunately, there are a few people who are so troubled in their feelings that they may abuse the children in their classrooms.

In the course of your school years, you will meet kind, patient teachers, angry, strict teachers, teachers who seem happy most of the time, teachers who are quiet and sad, teachers who yell at you or are unfair, and teachers who make the children in their classes feel that each one is a wonderful, lovable important person. It is important for you to understand that differences in teachers influence your work and your feelings about yourself.

While there are all these differences in the grown-ups around you, there is one thing that is very important. If there is anything happening in a classroom that you know is dangerous or wrong, you need to tell someone you trust, whether it is your parents or the school nurse, the principal or a counselor, or the gym teacher or anyone else you feel you can talk to.

Martin's parents had talked to him quite a lot about drugs and how dangerous they are and how you can tell when someone is taking drugs. Martin noticed that his teacher usually came to school acting calm and full of energy, but that by one or two o'clock in the afternoon Mr. Jeffrey's hands would be shaking, he would begin to sweat a lot, and he would get angry over unimportant things. Martin mentioned this to his parents who investigated at once, and the teacher was given a six-month leave of absence to go to a drug rehabilitation program.

Annie got very upset when she began to feel that her teacher was touching her too much. Other girls in the class joked about his "wandering hands," but Annie felt something was seriously wrong. She tried to tell her mother who just said, "Well isn't it nice you have such an affectionate teacher!" Annie got scared about going to school and when she had to go for her regular checkup she told her pediatrician why she was upset about school. The doctor called the school nurse who talked to the principal, and in this case it was necessary to dismiss the teacher after he had been carefully observed by the guidance counselor on the playground and in the school lunchroom.

Just like their students and everyone else, teachers have good days and bad, have private lives and problems. You are too often likely to feel that when a teacher is in a really bad mood it is the fault of you or your classmates. That's possible if the class has been on a tear! But when a teacher seems truly upset a lot of the time, it is not your fault. By the time you start going to school, you already know parents are human beings who are far from perfect; the same goes for teachers.

Parents' attitudes toward schools are also important. Some single working mothers are just too tired to visit their children's schools, while others feel that no matter how hard their lives may be, they must find some way to be in touch with the teachers, even if only by telephone. Some parents look upon schools as glorified baby-sitters, and other parents work very hard to improve schools through the PTA. They go to meetings to fight for better schools. Some parents want to supervise every homework assignment, others feel this is the child's responsibility and refuse to help. Some parents get all excited about what their children are learning, and at supper they ask lots of questions. Some families are so harassed, so "stressed-out," that not much attention is paid to what is happening in school.

If you are in a school where the curriculum is very demanding, where you are expected to learn things faster than you can, and where tests are given every week, you may become a nervous wreck. If you go to a school where the principal feels each teacher should decide when a child is ready for a new workbook, and he or she knows children learn best when they are not under pressure, you may feel calmer in school. If you go to a school where everyone is expected to do well in all the same subjects, chances are you may think of yourself as a failure; the abilities you have are just not the ones being tested in your schoolwork, and you think you will be stupid all your life. If you go to a school that includes classes in puppetry or ecology, or ancient Greek scientists and philosophers, or how to be a good baby-sitter, or how to write short stories, or how to grow a vegetable garden or weave rugs, chances are that if you are just "getting by" in some subjects, you will discover something that delights you and that you excel at. At the very same time that I would run and hide in the girl's bathroom at school when we were having a test in geometry and I didn't know a single answer, I was also starring in a play, because we had classes in theatre arts and I was a terrific actress. The more different kinds of classes, the more likely you are to find a place where you feel special and successful.

It is a myth—but a lot of people believe it—that all children can be good at all the same subjects. And another myth is that teachers can learn very important things about children from giving them tests—not true. All tests prove is that some children are better at taking them than others. Another myth is that a C is not a good mark. It may be that parents and teachers want you to get all A's and B's, but the truth is that most students get C's and grow up to be very successful people.

Let's think for a minute about your parents and relatives and neighbors. Do you know anyone who is good at everything? Is your father a failure because he still doesn't understand all the rules of grammar, although he has written fifteen very good books? Or how about your next-door neighbor, who has gone back to college and who tells your mother she gets so nervous that she gets terrible marks on tests, but she really knows the material. She says, "If they would only let me write an essay, they would see I understand. When I get multiple-choice questions, it takes me half an hour to figure out which answer comes closest to the truth, and I never finish." Does this make her a stupid person? Did you ever meet an "average" person? Is there any such thing? Every adult you know has both strengths and weaknesses and is never exactly like anyone else.

Real life in the grown-up world is very different from life in most schools. An example of this is in the matter of competition and cooperation. On the street where you live there might be several families that don't have money to buy the children winter clothes and shoes. One of the nicest things that can happen is that a group of neighbors decides to hold a bake sale to get money for these children's clothes. A cooperative neighborhood—even, we hope some-day, a cooperative world—is something we believe in. And yet in school if your friend, sitting next to you, tries to explain a problem on a test and is whispering or sending you a note, you will both be called to the principal's office, and probably your families will be called in to school and you will be labeled "cheaters." I believe that students should be encouraged to help each other, not only because they often learn more easily from each other but because school ought to be a place where we learn about caring for others. That to me would be the best preparation for becoming good citizens.

Some of the most special grown-ups do a lot of something that most teachers don't like at all—they daydream. My guess would be that when any valu-able invention occurs, the person who figured it out must have spent quite a lot of time just sitting and thinking his or her own thoughts. At one of the best universities there is a special honor given to one outstanding person in the arts or sciences—to spend a year thinking. The big question asked of this per-son as he or she moves into an office is, "Do you want your desk to face the outdoors, or do you have a favorite picture and would you prefer to face the wall?" Sitting and thinking one's thoughts is considered very important.

Did anybody ever ask you such a question in school? Many parents have mentioned to me that they have been told by a teacher, "Your child is wonderful in almost every way but I worry a lot because he/she sits and daydreams too much." Sometimes, of course, children daydream a lot because they feel unhappy and are troubled about something. Sometimes they are just bored and can't pay attention. But some daydreaming is the way to figure something out or to imagine new ways of solving problems.

You all know the things that help you to feel good about yourself—the time a teacher thanked you for being such a help or the time you worked so hard you finally understood something and a teacher said, "I'm so proud of you!" Or the time the whole class spent a Saturday afternoon cleaning out an empty lot full of junk and planting a few trees. Or the time someone in your class did such a good science project that you were all invited to a celebration in a science museum.

Probably the happiest and best moments in your school years happen when suddenly you understand something that has been confusing you for a long time, or when a teacher begins to read some poetry and you loved hearing it, and you go to the library and get some books of poetry. Or maybe the music teacher makes you work so hard you get angry—until the school chorus gets a standing ovation from parents at an assembly.

At their best today, schools can do much more than teach you the "three R's: reading, 'riting, and 'rithmetic." Schools can help you learn how to think about a problem; schools can teach you where to go to get information. Schools can help you learn how to get along with other people, how exciting an adventure learning can be.

However, because schools must be designed to teach all children many of the same skills, children whose ability to learn is at one extreme or the other, may have a difficult time. A learning-disabled child feels different from everyone else. A child who is a mathematical genius and ready for college mathematics in fifth grade feels strange and is an outcast. He or she is also bored. Some of the children who grow up to be the most interesting people we will ever hear about or know, have a hard time in school.

This can be the class comedian who is constantly being disciplined, who grows up to have his or her own television show. Or it can be a person we sometimes describe as "listening to a different drummer" or "having a special song to sing." This can be a young person whose thoughts and feelings go off in special and unusual directions. As a child, these people make other people uncomfortable. They are often loners; sometimes they are regarded as being stupid. When they grow up, it turns out they had an unusual and special talent that could not be fully understood or appreciated until the person grew up and made a medical discovery or became a Shakespearean actor, or wrote a best-selling novel, still in print thirty-five years later, or became an astronaut. The more unique a young person is, the more likely he or she will not have a comfortable time growing up, since most schools are not designed to deal with the unusual, the different, and most kids get a spooky feeling about such children.

And there you are, in the middle of all these variations and differences, trying so hard *not* to be special! You are in the middle of different teachers, different schools, different neighborhoods, and most of all, different students. And you all are trying so hard to be exactly like each other! The elementary and high-school years are the years when being popular is just about the most important thing on your mind. That's what makes it so hard to concentrate on homework! Will people like you even though you are very tall or very short? Will people ignore you because you learn new things slowly or don't have an athletic bone in your body? What must you wear to please your classmates? How can you get the attention and approval of the most popular girl or boy?

This is all a natural part of being young and insecure—uncertain about the future, not knowing what you will be like when you grow up, wanting to move away from parents and become closer to your own generation. It is also a period in which you will grow and change as much as you did during your first year of life. It is a slower growth period, but much more dramatic; nothing less than moving from childhood to the beginning of adulthood!

It is natural in all the confusion and uncertainty for you to struggle to keep your individuality a deep, dark secret. But when the struggle is hardest it would not be a bad idea to tell yourself that there is a time ahead when you will actually *enjoy* being a special self. When anyone says, "Oh, it's wonderful to be a child!" I feel like laughing. It's never as wonderful as being grown-up, when being special is a joyful fact of life.

Under most circumstances, and aside from serious problems, being a grown-up means you have a chance to make the most of who you really are. I'll tell you the truth: I was never as happy as a schoolgirl as I have been as an adult when I found out I could be myself—at last. No matter how strong the inclination may be for schools to standardize people, it never works—like those fingerprints that make you special all your life. While you try hard to be one of the crowd, I hope that there will be one small corner of your mind that says, "Hey, school is just to get me *started*, but after developing strong roots of knowledge, I will have the wings to fly my own course."

Chapter Five

THE WORLD AROUND US
❋

Julio lived in one of the poorest and most violent sections of New York City. His mother worked in a factory eight hours a day and spoke very little English. All his other relatives lived in Santo Domingo. Almost every day he heard about people being shot and killed because of drug wars; even little children were sometimes the innocent victims. When Julio was in fourth grade he began to realize that if he didn't join the street gang in his neighborhood he might get hurt by kids in rival gangs who attack anyone who enters their territory. Because he was so scared he stole some money from his mother's pocketbook and bought a sharp knife to protect himself. The fourth-grade class in his school was very overcrowded, and there were many troubled, unhappy children who could not get the attention they needed.

There were about twenty people in the gang in his territory, and they ranged in age from about eight to sixteen. Sal was tough and strong and the leader of the gang that provided the protection Julio felt he needed. Most of his gang could barely read or write. They often played hooky from school. Many of them had mothers who were working to support large families; many of them didn't know their fathers. Some had parents who were alcoholics or drug addicts, or both. Poverty, lack of education, poor nutrition, and serious emotional problems can lead to very self-destructive behavior in both adults and children.

When Julio was fifteen, his gang got into such a bad fight with a rival gang that one boy was killed, and Julio was sent to prison along with the others involved in the fight.

Up to that time the world in which Julio lived had been dangerous, frightening, and uncaring. In prison he met a minister who gave him more attention than he had ever gotten from any adult. The minister made him feel he was not really a bad person and that he could learn. Julio got his high-school equivalency diploma, and when he got out of prison at twenty his parole officer helped him get a job and go to college at night. Once in a very great while, prison can be a time of rehabilitation. The environment in which a young person lives can often be as important as heredity, family, or school.

I met Julio when he was a grown man. He was a social worker in a drug rehabilitation program. We talked about the terrible problems so many young people have, living in an environment in which they feel unloved, worthless, with no hope for the future. Julio said, "There are thousands—maybe even millions—of kids who feel as if they never should have been born because nobody wants them or cares about them."

Jacob lived in a much better neighborhood. His parents were able to pay close attention to him. Jacob was sent to one of the best public schools in the city, where he received a good deal of individual attention. He felt good about himself. And yet, although his situation was far better than Julio's, he too had some fears by the time he was in third and fourth grade. Some teenagers stole his bicycle when he was riding in the park. A coat was stolen out of his school locker. The main difference, however, between Jacob and Julio is that Jacob knew there were adults who would do everything they could to protect him. He could be afraid and upset about some of the things that happened to him but he did well in school. His parents were concerned about his health, his life, his future, his happiness, and he was surrounded by people who made him feel he would have a successful and happy future.

What kind of world do you live in? What makes you feel good about yourself? What things frighten you about the world? How do you feel about your future? Many of your feelings and ideas have been influenced by your surroundings and the life around you.

At thirteen Keesha is a wild person, always yelling, running, never sits still, can't concentrate at all. She doesn't trust anyone. She lives in an apartment building where there are lots of what her mother calls "crazy people." These are mostly drug addicts. Keesha has seen and heard every kind of violence since she was a toddler. At ten a man tried to rape her in the stairway, but she managed to push him hard, and she ran away. She never told anybody. When she was eleven, another girl started beating her up in the park and when Keesha screamed for help, nobody came to her rescue. Keesha's world is so frightening, so unbearable, that chances of Keesha becoming special in a good way are unlikely. In a different environment Keesha might have become a trusting, happy person.

Carl's father is in the army. Carl has moved so often that by the time he was in the ninth grade he'd been to four different schools. It's been very hard to adjust, and his schoolwork has suffered. He has no lasting friendships. If he had stayed in one place, he might have been a better student and made some good friends.

The environment in which each of us lives can greatly influence our personalities and our life experiences—how we become our special selves.

Scott's "natural temperament" from the day he was born was to be friendly, easygoing, unruffled. But living near a railroad track and an eight-lane highway, with constant noise and rumbling, made him nervous and tense much of the time. Roberta was an excitable, very physical child; she needed lots of space for outdoor play and roaming freely. Fortunately she was raised on a farm where she took care of animals, worked in the vegetable garden, and was free to run through the woods and fields. If she had lived in a crowded city where she could never go out alone to play, she might have become a most frustrated and unhappy person. The climate in which we live doesn't always have such a dramatic effect on a person—but it can.

A grandmother told me, "I think my grandson, Ramon, is a very worried child. I think he watches the TV news too much. We have relatives in Colombia (South America), and he listens to news about the drug wars there and how so many people are being killed. Then a child was killed in the cross fire caused by a fight between two drug sellers, and

I found him crying in his bedroom. This is such a terrible world for children!"

Jenna's father is a writer for television. He's very rich, and Jenna lives in Beverly Hills and goes to a private school. It often seems to her parents that her biggest worry is whether or not she has a pimple on her forehead. If you ask her if world problems bother her, she answers, "What problems?"

Naomi's grandparents were in a concentration camp in Austria during World War II. The stories of their terrible suffering and narrow escape have influenced Naomi's feelings about being Jewish. She finds it hard to trust people who are not Jewish. Unfortunately one of her ways of being special is to avoid making friends with any people who don't go to temple, which narrows her opportunities to learn about and enjoy people who belong to different religions or life-styles.

My early school days were spent during the years after World War I. When I began to read, we were given a series of books all about twins—Dutch twins and Chinese twins and twin children from many parts of the world. Our teachers and parents assured us there would never be another war. My parents and teachers were very idealistic. I was taught that world problems would be solved in my lifetime. I became an optimistic person, expecting the best in people, confident, hopeful, sure that human beings would become better and better. The streets of New York City were mostly clean and quiet then. I could play in the park and walk in the streets without ever being afraid. Neighbors were friendly.

I try to imagine how different the world must look to you. For one thing, there was no television when I was a child; it took a long time to hear bad news! Radio was just beginning and consisted mostly of music, comedians, and soap operas. I'm sure grown-ups worried about many things, but children were protected. Not once in my entire childhood did I ever hear about things like prostitution, drugs, the awful things happening to American Indians or to black people. Of course we never heard about atomic bombs or nuclear energy. The oceans, rivers, and earth were not poisoned. There were no chemicals yet invented to spray on fruits and vegetables; of course there were lots of mosquitoes and flies, which were annoying but not dangerous.

Can you imagine such a world? There are, unfortunately, too many ways in which you can feel justifiably frightened and insecure about your future. What is happening all over the world every day can upset you, make it hard for you to concentrate on schoolwork and discouraged about making any effort to accomplish anything. The state of the world and a sense of doom leads many young people who might otherwise be happy and optimistic to experiment with dangerous drugs, to listen to music that is so loud it makes it impossible to think, to be intrigued by dangerous games—even by the idea of suicide.

What I hope you will find in this chapter is that even in the worst of times people have always found ways to be special in a positive, creative way. During the great depression of the 1930's, President Roosevelt said, "The only thing we have to fear is fear itself." What he meant, I'm sure, was that people cannot give up during hard and dangerous times. What actually happened was that good things came from those hard times—social security, which may be helping your grandparents survive financially, or may be helping your neighbor's son who is mentally retarded get the special care he needs. Maybe your own father lost his job and was able to survive because of unemployment insurance.

Good things are happening right now; ten or fifteen years ago there were no city, state, or federal offices of environmental protection. There were no laws against companies that were producing acid rain and killing our trees and poisoning our lakes. There was no such thing as "Earth Day," when our whole country joined together to try to find solutions to problems of pollution. There is even a certain advantage in the fact that we *do* see everything that is happening in our cities and in the whole world. Once we know the facts we can begin to work on solutions.

Most of what I have been saying in this book has to do with each person being special. In some ways, a whole generation can be special—different from any other time.

I once asked a group of children what scared them the most on television. I thought they would mention some frightening, violent crime shows, but the first boy who answered said, "The news." I realized that of course he was right. The most frightening thing on television is the news programs. We are living in a time of confusion, fear, and frustration. Too many people are homeless. Too many people are drug addicts. Too many people can't find jobs. There are too many wars all over the world. We worry (quite rightly) about what price we might sometime have to pay for the energy we get from nuclear power plants. Too many people hate each other because of differences that make no sense at all. Too many cities have too many skyscrapers and too much traffic. Too much garbage has no place to go. Too many rivers, oceans, the very air we breathe, are becoming contaminated. We hear about dangerous chemicals in our food. Too many good leaders have been assassinated, too many of the people you want to admire—athletes, rock stars—turn out to be corrupt.

There have been many studies done to find out how young people feel, what they fear the most. A few years ago the greatest fear was of atomic war. More recently the greatest fear has been the destruction of our planet through terrible greed and neglect of our natural resources.

My husband tells me that every period of history has had terrible things happening, that life was really never any better than it is today. I suppose he is right, since he is a great student of history, but it still seems to me that many of the changes that have occurred since I was a child, more than sixty years ago, have made life much harder for your generation than was true of mine.

The things that trouble me the most occurred after World War II. It was a period of such rapid change that I am staggered by how different life has become. Small towns with attractive little main streets have just about disappeared, as enormous highways have been built. Small towns, with no buildings higher than three floors, have almost all disappeared and become big industrial cities with hundreds of factories, skyscrapers that shut out the sun and sky. Neighborhoods have almost disappeared, as has rural farm life. Most of us live in cities and suburbs where the traffic has become an insane daily problem. Too many trucks where there used to be freight trains. Too many enormous planes built to resemble cattle cars, too many airports where you have to walk a mile to catch a plane. These are all things that may seem perfectly normal to you but which upset me constantly.

When I was growing up, the people around me were hopeful. We believed life would get better, that most people were good. Life was not nearly as complicated, crowded, noisy, dirty, and stressful.

There were great fears; we worried about diseases for which there were not yet any vaccines or antibiotics (polio, diphtheria, smallpox, for example). Almost any serious illness or operation was much more dangerous. We were afraid of the problems we didn't yet know how to solve, but we were not usually as afraid of each other as human beings, partly because the population was much smaller. By the time World War II came along I was almost grown-up, and there were some terrible shocks ahead of me, but my childhood had been happy and untroubled by the outside world. Your lives have been quite different. From the time you were five or six, you had begun to hear about all kinds of social disasters, like Chernobyl or Love Canal, or massive and terrible oil spills, and underground toxic wastes seeping into drinking water.

If you are worried and scared it means you understand the situation! The world you live in is very complicated and has many serious problems, all of which you hear about. Imagine a world without radio or television or slick magazines or sensational newspapers. Imagine movies in which kissing had to be short and quick, where no adults could ever be seen sleeping in the same bed, when movie censors were so powerful that a movie could be banned for the use of even one swear word. Can you even imagine such a time? I can—I grew up in that kind of world. I wish you could too—not through censorship or pretending everything is perfect and romantic, but at least through not being bombarded twenty-four hours a day by pressures to buy junk food that is bad for you, or by movies and television shows depicting sex without caring or loving, or by showing scenes of people killing each other at a rate that is about ninety percent higher than in the real world.

Some very greedy and quite immoral people make money by having people on the telephone talk about sex in a way that may be exciting, but does not in any way suggest the kind of attitudes toward sex that can bring you any genuine pleasure. Too much sordid information can be very upsetting, especially to young children. A government that allows television stations to present programs in which people are having sexual intercourse—and even advertising places of prostitution—is, from my point of view, a country that does not truly care for its children.

Information is important, and I don't believe in lying to children, but I also believe that children are so impressionable that there are some things that are not suitable at an early age, and that adults need to fight against greedy people who make money through pornography, violent movies, recordings, and television. If it were up to me I would make laws against such people because of what they do to children.

Although so many things are painful, confusing, and frightening, there is also much to be said for not lying or overprotecting children from painful facts; you are not often "kept in the dark." Past generations of children had more vague anxieties because they were not told about sad things that might be happening around them, such as illness, financial problems, divorce, or death.

It is hard to be told about painful problems, but it is not nearly as upsetting as not knowing what is happening. My grandmother died when my mother was four, and she was told that her mother "was tired and had gone away for a vacation." Can you imagine how frightening and terrible that must have been? Her father was devastated, people were crying—how could they ever have thought they were "protecting" my mother? Like most other young children, she was sure her mother had left her because she was bad and unlovable. (Her mother had died in childbirth, at home, from a complication that would almost certainly be curable today.) She learned the truth a year later when she overheard a conversation between two neighbors. But no matter how she may have come to understand what had happened, she never completely got over this event because no one helped her to understand it. When children have nobody to talk to about frightening events they feel terribly lonely.

When my grandfather died I was not allowed to go to the funeral. I was not allowed to see anyone cry. I adored my grandfather, and it was not until I was about thirty and seeing a therapist that I was able to mourn for him. It was unfinished business. Now we understand that children need to have a chance to grieve, to feel their real feelings. When my grandmother died my daughter was only three, but I took her to the cemetery, and she saw me cry. She hugged me, and I told her I was very sad but her hugs helped me. She was learning at an early age that sad times can be lived through as long as people who love each other share their feelings.

There are so many good things about life today. Despite the fact that the news media tell us very little about it, more people are helping each other than ever before in history. There are self-help groups for parents, for the elderly, for alcoholics, drug addicts, battered women and children, for the mentally ill. There are schools that have counseling groups for children of divorce. There are self-help groups for widows and widowers, and for people who are disabled or have had serious operations. Even in prisons there are self-help groups to help the inmates understand how they became so angry and aggressive, able to hurt others because they had suffered so much hurt themselves.

As we realize the ways in which overpopulation and industrialization upset the ecology of the world, we are beginning to work at solving the problems they have created. There are many groups (like Greenpeace and the Sierra Club) and government agencies working on the problems, and people who own factories and oil tankers are beginning to realize they must take responsibility for dangers to the environment their businesses have caused.

One of the most important changes may seem strange to you. When I was a child there were separate benches, schools, bathrooms, and water fountains for white and black people all over the southern part of this country. The only black people allowed to appear in movies were singers, comedians, and servants. Now black people have become sheriffs, mayors, have run for governor and the presidency. Blacks can eat in any restaurant, stay at any hotel, sit anywhere in theaters. To someone my age this is more than I dared to hope for in my lifetime. Even though many black and white people still seem to hate each other for no other reason than the color of their skin, great changes are taking place.

There are now many new services for disabled people—special ramps, buses, elevators, or public rest rooms with stalls wide enough for wheelchairs. Disabled children now have a right to be part of regular classes in public school. At one time, like black people, they were segregated and discriminated against.

More than fifty percent of you have working mothers, many in careers that were unimaginable when I was growing up. A woman *fire fighter*? Unthinkable! A woman running for president or being the head of a bank or large corporation? Ridiculous! Fathers diapering babies and washing dishes? Impossible! Largely through the women's movement, more people have more choices than ever before in human history.

Perhaps most important of all, despite the fact that wars still occur, most of the people all over the world realize the stupidity, the futility of trying to solve problems this way.

You are living in a time when more people are struggling for freedom and democracy than ever before. If anyone had asked me twenty-five or thirty years ago if Germany would ever be reunited, or if Russia, Poland, or Czechoslovakia would give up communism or modify it greatly, I would have thought they were silly dreamers.

It's important to remember that rapid change—progress—can be very upsetting to people who feel insecure and who are frightened by new ideas. For awhile, it seems as if everything is getting worse, not better. But in the long run, I believe good changes will be accepted and bad ones defeated.

It is likely that you understand yourselves better than any earlier generation. There are books in every children's library, both fiction and nonfiction, that deal with psychology and feelings (see bibliography), and now there are counselors in school to help you with psychological problems. Teachers, camp counselors, and religious leaders are being trained to help both adults and children with personal and family problems. This was almost unheard of even fifty years ago.

What is special about your whole generation is that you know more than any other generation at your age. Some of what you know is disturbing, of course, but having a great deal of knowledge can also give you an opportunity to change the world. You know more about ecology than most adults; you know who the people are who are trying to save the dolphins and the whales. You know much more about people who are different, about people from other parts of the world; you know more about the ways in which people are alike. In any one of your classes, there may be people from Mexico, Puerto Rico, Yugoslavia, Russia, Cambodia, India—just about anywhere in the world. They are black, brown, red, white, yellow, and you are discovering what many grown-ups don't yet understand, that there are both wonderful people and pretty awful people in every group, and the only way to decide whom you like is by getting to know individuals. Bright, well-informed young people all over the world will bring new and better solutions to problems and will have a deep sense that there is no way to separate nations and governments anymore. Whatever happens influences all of us.

It is easy to feel frustrated, helpless, and even depressed about the problems you see around you. But there is only one very good way around this problem. We can live through painful and frightening times *if we take action.*

When my daughter was about nine years old there were many news reports about children in an African country, Biafra, starving to death. (By now you have undoubtedly heard many similar reports about different parts of the world.) My daughter became so upset she began to have nightmares and couldn't concentrate in school. We and our daughter joined in candlelight parades in front of the United Nations, protesting what was happening in Biafra. We found that there were people and groups sending food, blankets, and medicines to Biafra, and we collected these items ourselves and asked neighbors and friends to help. Our daughter gave some of her allowance to Biafran relief. The more we all got involved, the less upset she became.

My granddaughter cried when she saw lovely dolphins being caught in tuna nets. She and her mother sent money to organizations that were doing something about this. She told me to stop buying certain brands of tunafish; she gave me signs to put on my door, and pamphlets to send to my friends. Taking action made her feel less helpless.

Jade has many relatives in China, and she worries about how the government hurt and even killed many students. She wrote letters to the President and to her congressman protesting our supporting such a government. She is still sad and angry, but she also feels she is learning how people who care can begin to make a difference.

In a New Jersey town something very funny-smelling seemed to be seeping into the basements of almost all the houses in one neighborhood. It turned out that a chemical plant had used this area for dumping dangerous cancer-producing waste materials, before the homes were built. While parents fought to make the government do something to save their homes, the children were very frightened. When a sixth-grade class was discussing the problem with their teacher, Sophia asked Mr. Sloane if there were things people could do to protect themselves. Mr. Sloane thought that learning more about cancer prevention might be a very good class project. While steps were being taken by the town, the state, and the federal government to solve the problem, the sixth grade went to visit experts—doctors, nutritionists, and environmental groups—to get some facts about how they could protect themselves during this emergency. The children prepared leaflets, and they spoke at a school assembly. They made posters for the school hallways: "DON'T PLANT ANY VEGETABLE GARDENS," "EAT PLENTY OF FRUIT," and "WASH THOROUGHLY AFTER PLAYING OUTDOORS." The situation was very scary but doing something useful had helped this class surmount their fears.

The more young people can participate in doing good works, the more they can feel hopeful and proud. Some schools give students special credit for after-school activities, such as visiting children in a hospital, or old people in a nursing home to play checkers or chess or just sit and talk. In one school a seventh-grade class made up a musical show and performed it at several local nursing homes. A number of nursing-home directors have encouraged school children to visit and bring their pets with them.

Young people can keep a watchful eye out for many problems. Kerry can see an apartment-house smokestack from her window, and whenever there is black smoke pouring out she calls the city environmental protection agency. Gerald was at home with a cold one day and heard a lot of noise and children crying in a next-door apartment; he told his parents about it, who were at work all day and hadn't noticed. The next time they heard it, they called the police. It turned out that two children were being abused. A fourth-grade class in a New England school started to count the number of dead trees in a nearby state park. They decided to try to find out just how serious the problem of acid rain was in their state and asked for appointments with the senators and congressmen in their district. They wrote a report which, they were promised, would be sent to the proper government committees. Some things that happen can be discouraging, but getting involved can make good things happen.

The environment can give you a good start in life or it can give you burdens you cannot carry. Your personal experiences can help you to become strong enough to deal with whatever problems you may have to face. If you get help at home and in school to see yourself as a competent, worthwhile person, you will be able to take action even when you are very young, and that will give you a feeling of hope and pride. If parents, teachers, and other adults talk to you openly and honestly about all the upsetting things you see and hear, you will be better able to take them in stride; the less adults help you to understand and accept your feelings, the more difficult it will be for you to solve problems. The most-effective way to solve problems is to work at discovering what it is that you and your friends can do about issues that you think need fixing and changing.

Anisa was her most unique self when, using her natural gift for drawing, she made a poster having to do with recycling cans and newspapers; Raphael had a natural talent with words, and he and a friend made up a rap song for a school assembly about race relations. Michael decided that when he grew up he wanted to discover some way to reuse plastic containers, and he began to work hard in his chemistry class and took out lots of books from the library, so that someday he could go to a good university where such research was going on.

There are also some not very helpful ways of being special. One can get furious at the unfairness of life and want to hurt other people. Anger helps people to forget. While Russell was beating up little kids and stealing their lunch money and starting to smoke marijuana, he was able to forget his own troubles for awhile. People who become alcoholics or drug addicts—or even burglars or murderers—are people who have given up on themselves and have no hope at all; their anger can turn against themselves or against others.

When I was in college I had a professor who was teaching us how different people in different parts of the world think and behave. One day he told us that there was a small island in the Pacific with a village where there was only one place to get fresh water. Everyone had to come to this faucet to get water. The people on this island had a way to decide if a person was sane or insane. When someone began to behave strangely they would bring that person to the water faucet. There would be a bucket under the faucet. The water would be running, spilling over the sides of this pail. Nearby was a large ladle, a giant-size soupspoon. This person would be told, "You see, we have a problem. All the water is being wasted. What should we do about it?" If the person took hold of the ladle and tried to use it to empty the bucket, he would be judged as insane. If, on the other hand, he turned off the faucet, he was congratulated on being wise as well as sane.

What has this story got to do with you and the world in which you live? Just about *everything*! My

hope is that when you grow up and you see a problem, you will not try to solve it in an easy and useless way. What I hope you will think about is how
you can *solve* the problem—turn off the faucet. For
example, if homeless people are put in shelters, that's
ladling. Building new, moderately priced housing is
a way to turn off the faucet. Ladling is always an
overly simple answer to a very complicated problem. Sending teenagers who get into trouble to prison
is ladling. In order to turn off the faucet we would
have to see that these young people got the best
possible help through excellent schools and teachers, through counseling, and experts working with
their parents to help them understand their children
better. We can never solve problems in a simple,
superficial way.

If a child seems to have a learning problem that
no one can figure out, it would be ladling to punish
this child by giving twice as much homework.
Turning off the faucet would involve special-educa-
tion teachers—maybe even something as sensible as
seeing to it that the child had a good breakfast every
morning before coming to school, so he or she would
not be too tired to think. Hiring more fire fighters
and police officers is a form of ladling, because it
doesn't solve the problems of fire and crime. Old
tenements are going to burn down, miserable angry

people are going to commit crimes. To turn off the faucet you could build new fireproof apartment buildings, and provide all the things children need in order to grow up without severe emotional problems, which may encourage them to become criminals. Turning off the faucet would mean spending a lot of money on good schools instead of on prisons.

See if you can think of the things people do that are ladling (and don't solve problems) and things that show we are trying to turn off the faucet. A teacher who yells at a child for being confused and not knowing an answer is ladling. A teacher who tries to find out if this child needs glasses is turning off the faucet. If there is a bully in your class and your dad wants to teach you how to box, that's ladling. If your parents try to understand why this bully is unhappy and find some way to help, that's turning off the faucet. I suppose one of the easiest ways to look at solving problems is: If you broke a leg and the doctor were to give you some aspirin— that's ladling! Your leg would still be broken. Turning off the faucet (solving the problem) would be to take an X ray and set your leg in a cast—and fix the hole in the road where you tripped!

Throughout my adult life, I have thought about that little village and the bucket of water. It has helped me to understand why problems are too often not solved—and what has to be done to make real and lasting changes. Perhaps this story can help you too. The most special we can be is to find answers to our problems that can truly change our lives.

Chapter Six

BECOMING YOUR OWN BEST FRIEND

Nobody can become his or her own most-special self without having one particular best friend. By some strange coincidence this friend has your name and looks exactly like you! Throughout your whole life there will be times when you will have to make decisions, choices; often these will require understanding yourself, liking yourself—yes, even loving yourself. The way to become your most special self requires that you be your own best friend.

Before I mention some adults who learned to make the most of their own internal friend, I suggest you look around you and do a little test. Which grown-ups in your life can you tell are the most happy with themselves? Which people don't strike you as being really individual, unique people? Which adults seem to you to be the happiest people you know?

When I look back to my own childhood, the first name that pops into my head is Aunt Lillie. Boy, was she special! She wanted more than anything else in the world to be a dancer. She was a member of a small dance group, but never once did she earn any money dancing. Her group wore strange Grecianlike chiffon flowing robes. They believed in performing a classical kind of dancing that had been done three thousand years ago in Greece. They had a few students, and they ran a summer camp for the children of the members of their "School of Rhythm." When my husband and I and our daughter went to visit the camp we had to wear costumes too. Aunt Lillie died in her eighties. All of her adult life she worked at very poor-paying jobs or ones that she wasn't very good at. She never had fancy clothes; she drove old, secondhand cars; she lived alone, usually in one or two rooms; she never married or had any children. When she was about to die she told my husband, "I have had a wonderful life—dancing, dancing."

How we children adored her! Her lovely tinkling laugh still rings in my ears, and she was the best storyteller I ever knew. Her life was the most different from anyone I can think of, and she was the happiest person I knew. "I listen to the inner songs in my heart," she would say.

And then there was Uncle Simon. His father owned

a clothing factory, and by the time he was fifteen he began working there. The business became very successful; he and his father and brothers made a lot of money. He married and had children. All I remember about him is his sad face and that his children had many problems growing up. It is difficult to describe him—just a very quiet man, never mean, never loud—never much of anything. It's as if he could have been any one of a thousand other businessmen. After he retired, when he was quite old, he moved to Arizona. His apartment was next door to a small restaurant, and he became close friends with the owner. After awhile Simon asked if he could help out on busy days, waiting on tables, slicing roast beef, making potato puddings. His wife and brothers thought he was crazy—they said he was too old, and such hard work would make him sick. My only memory of Uncle Simon is the one time I saw him when he made me a sandwich in the restaurant. It was a sandwich he invented called "The Richard Tucker Sandwich." He told me he loved the opera and Richard Tucker had been his favorite tenor. He said, "You may not believe this but when I was a young man I wanted to study singing. I was always too busy." I was so glad I had had the chance to see Uncle Simon being his special self at the end of his life.

Who is the most unusual person you can think

of? Is it the baseball coach at school who would rather be with "his kids" than take a vacation? Is it an aunt who plays the flute in a community orchestra while she's raising five children, and her house is always a mess? Is it your mother, perhaps, who constantly complains about how hard it is to "do ten jobs at once," but you notice that every time she comes home from her computer training course, she seems happy and refreshed? And can you think of people you know whom you can't think of any special way to describe? They just seem to melt into the background and could be any one of a dozen other people.

Enjoying life doesn't mean that a person is happy all the time. I have never met or heard of such a person! Everyone has problems of one kind or another—worries, failures, arguments with other people. Everyone goes through times of feeling anxious and depressed. Life is full of challenges and even great suffering at certain times, such as the serious illness of a child, the death of a grandparent, unemployment, misunderstandings with friends and relatives. The kind of happiness I mean is that deep inside me there is the feeling that no matter how hard life may be, I am doing the things that make me a special person and my own best friend.

Since the decisions you will someday be making about your own adult life are still far in the future,

I'd like to tell you about a few examples of the choices that were made by grown people when they finally became their own best friend.

Andy was always a nice, kind person. He has a wife and two grown sons. For twenty-five years he worked as a cashier in one bank or another. He was never promoted, and he lost his job three or four times, but always found some other bank that would hire him because he had a nice, pleasant personality; people liked him and he never made any trouble.

Andy lost his last job when he was fifty-five years old, and then he was really scared. He had to begin to face the fact that he had always hated the work he was doing and he could never, ever, do it well or work steadily. His wife was a brave and loving woman. She said, "We will somehow manage to live on my salary at the library, while you think about what you would like to do."

While Andy tried to figure out what he could do well and would enjoy doing, a friend gave him a job three mornings a week as an assistant clerk in his office. Andy found that he kept going for long walks on the beaches and always ended up in the harbor of his town talking to fishermen. He lived in a seacoast town where there were many tourists in the summertime. Some of the men taught him how to go crabbing, and after awhile he began selling the crabs on the dock. He met a man who spent the summers taking fishing parties out. He met another man who told him that people were getting more and more interested in taking boats out to look at whales. Andy began to realize he had never been so happy in his whole life. At first he offered to help anyone who needed any assistance on the sight-seeing or fishing boats. After awhile he asked for paying jobs. He never earns very much, and he and his wife have to continue to live simply, but Andy is the success he always wanted to be. No one who joins him on any of the boats ever forgets him. He tells terrible jokes and he plays with the children and he makes everyone feel safe even if they hit bad weather. He's special.

Miriam wanted to get married and have a family. Just before she met her husband, Douglas, she spent a summer after college at a summer theater, painting scenery, playing walk-on parts, singing in the chorus. She had never been happier in her whole life. Then she met Douglas, and fell in love and got married. She worked as a secretary and a saleslady for awhile until her first child was born, and then she decided to stay at home and be a homemaker and a mother. She and Douglas had four children. Miriam enjoyed what she was doing, and her life appeared to be quite perfect to other people. What a surprise it was to those of us who knew her to see what she did after she had become a grandmother and had her sixty-fifth birthday. "That's *it!*" she seemed to be saying, "Now it's my turn." She began taking acting classes; she hired a voice coach. She began doing aerobic exercises to get herself in shape. She joined various theatrical unions and started going to calls for extras in movies. She tried for parts in television advertising.

After three years she decided the chances of getting enough work were most unlikely, so she joined a volunteer group of older actors who go to senior citizen centers and put on plays. They began to do so well that the park commissioner asked them to put on some plays for kids in a park amphitheater.

Miriam was always a nice person and seemed to be content but she wasn't ever the kind of person you noticed a lot. It was hard to see her as distinct or different at a PTA meeting or as a Cub Scout leader. At the age of seventy she is having the time of her life and has more energy than anyone can remember her ever having had before. Anyone who sees her perform sees a very special person. She certainly got to be her own best friend.

Alberto had a very hard time in elementary school and left high school as soon as he was sixteen. He had come to live in New York from Puerto Rico, lived in a poor neighborhood, went to an over-crowded school, and almost immediately he began to be labeled by teachers as not being too bright. He was scared and shy and confused and he began to live up to this picture that others had of him.

By the time he was twenty, he was in jail for forging checks. While he was in prison he was surprised to find out there was a teacher who came twice a week to teach prisoners to read. He got excited about what he was learning. He found some mathematics books in the prison library and discovered he could understand the problems and that he loved working with numbers. Another inmate told him about The Fortune Society and that when he got out they would give him tutors so he could pass his high-school equivalency and get a job. Alberto had not really ever had a chance to be his own best friend before. He hated the self that people considered stupid and cowardly. Strangely enough, with time on his hands, in prison he had begun to realize he wasn't stupid at all, and now it became possible to want to be a friend to himself. Alberto is now thirty-five years old. He is going to school at night to become a certified public accountant while he works for a businessman who decided to give him a chance as an assistant to the company's comptroller. He works so hard and is so good at his job that he has become a very special person. It took learning to like himself a lot.

Irene had a terrific job at an advertising firm; she

made a lot of money. But she began to have migraine headaches. She went to see a psychiatrist who helped her to think of herself, as an important person. Irene went back to school to become a physical therapist. Now she works with disabled children. She loves her work, and on only half the salary she made before. The children think she is really something special.

One of many families I have known in the past twenty years, at a time when young people began to rebel against doing what was expected of them, is the Kingman family. The father is a doctor, the mother is a psychologist. They certainly expected their two sons to go to college and choose a profession. Arnold wanted to please his parents. He went to dental school, got married, had two kids. That's the last anyone heard of Arnold until he began drinking too much and got a divorce. People said, "Just like a lot of other men." Felix, his younger brother, refused to go to college. He thought he was breaking his mother's heart and felt bad, but could not stop himself. He took the money he got in gifts for his high-school graduation, bought an old jalopy, and began traveling all over the United States, mostly getting jobs as a dishwasher or short-order cook in roadside restaurants. At one time he ended up picking cherries, at another he pumped gas. His father could hardly bear to hear what Felix was doing.

Both parents worried all the time. "What have we done wrong?" they asked themselves.

What they realized much later was that Felix had somehow managed to become his own best friend at an early age. Before he settled down he wanted to find out what he could do; could he take care of himself? What kind of people did he like the best? Was he a city person or a country person? Did he like to work with other people or alone?

Two years after he began traveling he wrote to his parents that he was coming home. Now he felt ready to go to college. He wanted to become an anthropologist, a person who studied interesting groups of people in different parts of the world. Ten years later he has written a book that has become a best-seller, about his living with a group of South American Indians. He has been asked to give speeches at important conferences. His book is now used in many colleges. He's a special person—but it took a lot of courage and struggle to get there.

Being a special person is not the same as doing something special. It has nothing at all to do with becoming a performer or a great scientist or making a lot of money. I know a nursery-school teacher who has been in the same school for fourteen years, does not get paid a high-enough salary for the important work she does, but is doing exactly what she wants to do. I once had a long trip in a taxi where the driver told me stories about the interesting people he met and how proud he was that he knew every street in his city. "I just love my job," he said. On a plane trip I sat next to a man who was a baker in a pastry shop who seemed so delighted when I asked some questions and he could describe some of his specialties. All over this country there are people whose names you will never hear, whose lives you may never know about, but who have found their own special talents and interests, whatever they may be—police officers, fire fighters, train conductors, shoe salespeople, reporters, house painters, carpenters, plumbers, car mechanics. They wake up every morning happy to be doing what they do. What is most important is that whatever kind of work and life we choose, we need to feel, "This is my niche in life, this is where I belong."

You are just on the threshold of having to think seriously about what is special about yourself. It is probably too early for you to even want to think about it, because being special isn't what you want, right now. But it will help you a lot later on if once in awhile you allow yourself to dream about the future. When I was young I often found myself lying in bed pretending that I was a teacher, talking to little children. When I grew up I found that I wanted to talk to children of all ages—and here I am, doing just that! At the time I allowed myself to pretend, what I *thought* I wanted was to look like Christine, be smart in French class, like Gloria, play hockey like Maureen, and have the boys crazy about me, like Lorraine. The last thing I wanted was to be Eda! Now I'd rather be Eda than anyone else, but it took a long time to want to be my special self.

Some children have very ambitious parents with big dreams for their child's future. They start pushing too hard, when a child is very young, for him or her to become special. There are mothers who enter a beautiful baby in a beauty contest, fathers who insist that a son or daughter start to ride horseback long before the child is interested or can have any satisfying success. There are mothers or fathers who decide that their child has "a perfect body for ballet" and start lessons when the child wants to be out playing after school.

When a child is old enough to speak up and demand to do what comes naturally, it may be that too much time has been wasted in unnecessary suffering and failure. What can a young child, still completely dependent on parents, loving them a lot and not wanting to hurt their feelings, do?

You can speak up. Not shouting or yelling or crying but saying, "I need to tell you how I feel," or, "Don't we all think it's great when a person can do something he or she loves? I'm not ready yet to know what that might be." Or if that's too hard to say, just ask for more time—just say it makes you feel unhappy, upset, to be doing too much of something you are not sure is the right thing for you to do. If parents insist on piano lessons, see if you can work out a deal: one year of piano, and a second year of the guitar. Or if a mother feels she must make up for a dad who isn't at home anymore, and can't bear it if you don't practice catching in the backyard every Saturday, try to make a deal: one Saturday for baseball practice, the next Saturday at the library or a museum.

One problem is that most young people feel that if they don't do exactly what their parents want them to do the parents will be angry and disapproving or miserable, and the child is being cruel and unfeeling. Not true in most cases. When Arnold thought he'd die if his parents told him once more how wonderful it would be after going to a graduate school in business administration so that he could work for his father (when he already knew he would have to do *something* where he could draw and write books like Dr. Seuss), he finally said, "Did you ever hear about the book about Auntie Mame? Remember the movie? Remember how you laughed and thought she was so great? Well she said life was a banquet and anyone would be a fool not to try everything. Don't you want me to do that?"

Arnold's parents were astounded by this statement. They began to laugh. Every time they would start to advise Arnold about what he should study and what his major should be in college, he would yell, "It's banquet time!"

But for many young people the struggle to search for what is most special about themselves can meet with strong opposition—not because most parents and teachers are cruel or unfeeling, but because they believe they know what is best to help a child become successful and happy. Or they may be afraid the young person will do something foolish or dangerous. Working for the peace corps or any other group parents respect may be a way of testing oneself in relative safety. You can talk and explain your feelings, but if you are unable to change the minds of the most important adults around you, you can still keep an *open mind*—you can be thinking your own thoughts, preparing yourself for the time when the choices will be your own. I found that writing stories and keeping a diary helped me to begin to express my deepest feelings and hopes without arguments, without feeling I was disappointing anyone. I kept these secret writings and reread them many times as I grew up. I'm astounded when I look at them now (at the age of sixty-eight!) that so much of what I felt still seems to be true for me.

Another important way to try many different dishes at the "banquet of life" is to ask parents, grandparents, teachers, to allow you opportunities for different kinds of experiences, trying to make the point that you are an adventurer, that you are not disregarding the possibilities that your family wants for you, but that you think it will help you to have many different experiences first.

Marshall's parents feel that life has become much too competitive at school and on the playing fields. They think children should do things they enjoy doing without competing with others. Marshall wants to go to the camp where his best friend is going. The camp emphasizes competitive sports; no art classes, no nature walks—just athletic activities and playing to win. They are very distressed by Marshall's wanting this kind of experience. But Marshall tells them he just wants to *try it once,* and that he may change his mind. He wants to go to several different kinds of camps in the next few years. Maybe he can set his parents' minds at ease.

Audrey's parents suffer every time she fails at anything. They are so afraid she will get the idea she's not good at anything. The truth is that Audrey is just the kind of kid who loves a challenge—she thinks it's just great to dare to take some risks and see what happens. The clumsier she is, the more she wants to try figure skating; the worse her accent the more she wants to study Russian as well as French; the more she realizes she has two left feet, the more she wants to try the relay races. The truth is she's a happy person who likes herself. Somehow she has to try to relieve her parents' worries, let them know that adventure is more important than her winning or losing.

When you grow up and have to make decisions about your own specialness, there are certain qualities you will need. One of these is inner discipline—learning to stick to a task and see it through, no matter how hard or discouraging it may be. Another quality is flexibility—realizing when you have to adapt or change your goals sometimes. And perhaps most of all, you will need to have the courage of your convictions. And that's the bottom line. In order to have the courage to stand up for what you feel you need, what can provide you with joy and fulfillment, you will have to like yourself as much as Andy and Miriam and Felix and Uncle Simon and Aunt Lillie.

When you begin the exciting search into what makes you different from anyone else, what makes you know you are your own best friend, you will need to have come to understand yourself pretty well, to have had wide experiences in many different undertakings, and to like yourself as much as you can ever like anyone. Much of this work still lies ahead of you, but you can begin to prepare yourself.

Try to tell yourself that you have a friend whom

you like very much. This friend needs a lot of help becoming more confident, developing strong ideals and goals. This is a friend who gets scared, who worries, who needs to learn to fail and try again. This is a friend who needs to know other people respect and care for her or him—a friend who needs time to grow and to change. And then tell yourself that this friend is you.

Further Reading

On Heredity:

Fradin, Dennis. *Heredity: A New True Book*. Chicago: Children's Press, 1987.

Hofstein, Sadie. *The Human Story: Facts on Growth and Reproduction*. Glenview, Illinois: Scott, Foresman and Co., 1967.

Patent, Dorothy Hinshaw. *Grandfather's Nose: Why We Look Alike or Different*. New York: Franklin Watts, 1989.

On the First Five Years:

LeShan, Eda. *What Makes Me Feel This Way?* New York: Macmillan, 1972.

On the Family:

LeShan, Eda. *What's Going to Happen to Me? When Parents Separate or Divorce*. New York: Macmillan, 1978.

LeShan, Eda. *When Grownups Drive You Crazy*. New York: Macmillan, 1988.

On the School Years:

LeShan, Eda. *When Kids Drive Kids Crazy*. New York: Dial Books for Young Readers, 1990.

On the World Around Us:

Greenfield, Eloise. *Night on Neighborhood Street,* illus. by Jan Spivey Gilchrist. New York: Dial Books for Young Readers, 1991.

LeShan, Eda. *The Roots of Crime*. New York: Four Winds, 1981.

Meltzer, Milton. *Crime in America*. New York: Morrow, 1990.

———. *Poverty in America*. New York: Morrow, 1986.

———. *Starting From Home*. New York: Viking Penguin, 1988.

Meltzer, Milton, and Langston Hughes. *African American History, Four Centuries of Black Life*. New York: Scholastic, 1990.

About the Author

Eda LeShan is a well-known author and columnist who has written over twenty books on various aspects of family relationships. Her most recent book for young readers, *When Kids Drive Kids Crazy* (Dial) was said by *School Library Journal* to "hit the mark, [and to be] a useful, practical, and very readable guide on interpersonal relationships." Among her other books are *Learning to Say Goodbye: When a Parent Dies* and *When Grownups Drive You Crazy*. Mrs. LeShan, an educator and family counselor for many years, has also appeared as a guest on *Good Morning America*, *The Today Show*, and the *Donahue* show, among others.

Mrs. LeShan received the Karl Menninger Award from the Fortune Society. She also received the Distinguished Alumnus Award from Teachers College, Columbia University, and the Mothers of America Award. She lives with her husband in New York City.